SWARAJ AT 58

Kusay. Sabunwala

First published in 2018 by

Becomeshakespeare.com
Wordit Content Design & Editing Services Pvt Ltd
Unit - 26, Building A-1, Nr Wadala RTO, Wadala (East),
Mumbai 400037, India
T:+91 8080226699

This book has been funded by WORDIT ART FUND
WORDIT ART FUND helps deserving
Authors publish their work
To apply for funding, please visit us at
becomeshakespeare.com

©
ISBN: 978-93-88081-57-3

1

Jana Gana Mana..

The air reverberated with the rousing strains of the National Anthem, after the Prime minister of India delivered his 'Tryst with destiny' speech to the nation from Delhi's constituent assembly.

It was 15th August 1947 and every nook and corner of the country was participating joyously in the birth of Independent India.

By end-June streaks of lightening, ferocious thunder and ominous dark clouds hovering over the sky signal the advent of monsoon over most of North India. This year the July's rains had been bountiful almost as if gods seemed in a jolly good mood and they too were celebrating the rise of new dawn. The people too reciprocated by dancing unabashedly and paying obeisance to rain gods.

August is a peak monsoon month. But on Independence Day, Gods, it seemed willingly spared the day with no showers, the sun was shining like amber the brightness dispelled the dark clouds of British Raj.

In a non-descript, standard Indian village, hard to find on the map. The narrow paths were filled with dust and gravel. The silence and sleepiness of village life would get disturbed by periodic gust of winds, blowing the dust in a whirl and whistle and flustering the leaves like tinkle of tin scraps. The place where time stood still; over there stood the mud house of Kishen Goswami, fondly called Kisna.

His house was an exemplary village farmer's decrepit hut with mud walls, a leaking roof, no furniture or toilet. Inside wooden planks had been inserted into the hollow spaces in the walls to create shelves to store house wares and clothes, serving as open closets. The clothes were tied in a piece of cloth and bundled like a ball, placed in these closets. There was no separate kitchen neither the utensils, the scattered earthen ware were used as pots and pans with just a crude open chullah and beside it was a small pipe for blowing and fanning up the flames.

The house (or call it a hut) was in such dire state that the mud walls had developed hairline cracks even though they were regularly re-plastered with cow dung to hold them in one piece. During thunderstorms and incessant rainfall the walls would shake and shiver to such an extent that it endangered the very survival of the house.

Outside the hut there was an enclosed courtyard where Kisna's only other possession other then land were a fractured charpoy which was placed in the centre, its legs tied and held tight with frayed ropes. In the barn at the side were two buffaloes tied to a post while six goats and handful of chicks roamed around. The barn ground was littered with hay, cow pats and goat turds.

Yet in those caste conscious days his position was still considered better as he was an upper caste Brahmin and sole owner of ten acres of single intact piece of land, in a country where land holdings are sparse and fragmented.

His parents died when he reached marriage able age, while his uncles and their families had migrated as indentured labor a long time ago. He had two brothers and two sisters. Two sisters were married off and settled in nearby villages, one brother died of mysterious illness while he was an adolescent and his elder brother was killed fighting for British troops during World War II and cremated at a far-away place. Cremated or buried was quite contentious as nobody in their village or anyone from another village had laid any claim for their dead ones neither was anybody compensated for the dead and so as it remained. They were the fodder of British army and dispensed as collateral damage to their war ambitions. So Kisna was fortunate to own those ten acres of land.

Kisna's hut was situated on the edge of the village, on the way towards city, far from the other huts that were clustered together. As a result his land adjoined his dwelling, unlike the other farmers who lived in the village and had farmlands some distance away.

****

In the courtyard Kisna was sitting on his haunches, his chin cupped in his palms, nervously shaking his legs as he waited expectantly for the birth of his child.

Kisna was fair but skin had tanned to pale gold due to unforgiving sunshine. He was of medium height, dressed in impeccable and crisp white dhoti and kurta with matching white turban. He had only three pairs of cloth a time that he would rigorously wash to wear it alternatively. He kept his wear neat and clean.

All his relatives had gathered at his house. The poor man's relatives are not expected to be dressed nobly, unlike him their clothes appeared smudged, tattered and wrinkled a clear indication of their impoverished condition. Kisna although being same shined with clean clothes like dove among crows easily distinguishable amongst the lot.

While Kisna sat with utmost care, dusting his space before taking a seat, his relatives were carelessly sitting spread-legged, casually spread eagled on the ground or were squatting in the courtyard or on charpoy waiting in anticipation.

The mid-wife rushed around frantically, carrying hot water, piece of cloth, some medicinal leaves, herbs and paste to bring comfort to Rani, Kisna's wife who was about to deliver, with every cry of pain the anxiety would deepen.

It was early morning, the hour of day's break. Every day, the morning march by children (Prabhat Pheri) would pass by Kisna's house. Prabhat Pheri had an interesting beginning. The British Raj had become intolerable and Indians were contributing in whatever way they could with their agitation against the colonial power. The children decided not to be left out and came up with a novel way to hold peaceful token protest by carrying out morning march against the Raj, the young girls in polka dotted frocks and boys in half pants with placards in hands and passion for freedom in their hearts. They would walk in a

4

neat row of four or five and by raising their clinched fists would slogan for the call of Independence.

There were but on a different pitch today. They were happily waving the Indian tricolor chanting new slogan "India is Independent", "India is Independent", "Swaraj is here". The air resounded with the sound of their voices.

Everyone at Kisna's house watched the procession go by. And to Kisna a name clicked on hearing the word Swaraj, he thought it would be the perfect name for his newborn (provided it was a boy).

Suddenly there was a shrill from behind. The mid wife raised the child high up in her arms like a prized trophy and announced. "Congratulations, you are a father to a son, a son that has brought happiness not only to you but to all of us. He is born in a free country."

For Kisna, his happiness was enhanced by the fact that his son had been born at such a historically significant moment. His relatives erupted with joy and went into frenzy. The place came alive akin to Holi fervor, they smothered gulal on one another and by beating utensils and drums they begun to dance wildly.

In the midst of this revelry, one person exclaimed, "Where are the sweets?"

The other one strained his neck from behind prodding on the shoulder of the one in front of him. He shouted excitedly, "Go, go, dear, bring sweets, the mere mention makes my mouth water."

Kisna left them dancing and went to a village market to purchase sweets.

The shopkeeper at the sweet meat mart was talking to his chief sweet preparer Anwar Miyan who had come to bid him farewell.

"Don't go please; you are the best sweet preparer around."

Anwar Miyan, "Malik, I have my relatives and a cousin in Lahore, some months back he came to the village. He appeared a bit disoriented with the events happening back at his place and I asked him about it and this is what he said 'Brother the situation is getting out of control; from sometime back the freedom movement has lost its direction. Muslim League is gaining ground with their ideologies and is finding support among the Muslim stronghold. They are rendering spiteful and divisive speeches; hatred for other community is boiling. Hindus are viewed with scorn. Time has become so desperate it is better to be on a safe side, be with the majority. Muslims are stockpiling their houses with sticks, sickles, knives, swords, pick-axe, homemade pistols and what not sort of weaponry.'

"I had but dismissed his talks as he has a tendency to exaggerate. But as of now I have got the news that in the nearby city the same thing is happening. Hindus are getting armed to preempt an attack or probably for retaliation. This atmosphere is not conducive for our stay, otherwise, who makes the choice to relocate? A line on paper and lust of power of few decides the fate of the rest of us humans. We are no more than herds of cattle forced to flee in the direction that others have decreed is our new home.

It looks unlikely but if given a chance I'll surely stay not leaving my land, ancestry, childhood reminiscences and roots."

Kisna was intently listening to their conversations.

Anwar Miyan had a thick beard and he wore a long kurta.

Kisna for first time minded that they both wore kurta but it was the length that was different. His kurta was short and up to the thighs and Anwar Miyan's kurta was long and below the knees but leave aside the long and short of it. Kisna wondered that how he everyday in his life had seen the wear but never with the prism of a hindu kurta or a muslim kurta but as a simple Indian attire, but today the change appeared strikingly apparent. The situation had changed so drastically that in an instant a similar wear appeared different. Kisna twisted his perception to observe that there were more similarities in their wear and widely altering from sahib's attire.

Suddenly, to some Anwar Miyan's presence became noticeable, irritable and unwarranted.

By this time they all saw Shambu coming sprinting from the city's side. Shambu paused for breath and Kisna enquired, "What's the matter, Why are you perspiring and in such a hurry?"

Shambu carried news from one place to another for a charge. Banne Nawab had heard of a rumour that a Muslim royal family in the city had been looted and forced to flee the country and some of his family members were slaughtered, he wanted to confirm the news, so today Shambu was acting as an emissary to Banne.

He was on his way to Banne zamindar. He eyed towards Anwar Miyan and gestured, "Miyan it is better that you pack up and move fast or you would be hunted by pack of wolves on a prowl. The people in the city have turned pyromaniacs; burning and looting, no trace of decency or humanity is left." He just hinted him, didn't stop for his reaction and departed.

The shopkeeper was speechless, he no more found the courage to argue or reason Anwar Miyan. Anwar Miyan, reading the situation, swiftly whisked away from the scene.

At that same time a crowd started to assemble at the crossroads of village, holding long and sturdy bamboo sticks. They were engrossed in serious discussions. It looked as if bloodshed was imminent. Independence had brought with it the partition of the sub continent into two new nations and the scene was about to turn ugly and terrifying.

The shopkeeper turned to Kisna and said, "Independence doesn't seem to come easy to us. The British have done their last bit of damage, before departing they have left a permanent scar on our mother earth."

Kisna nodded his head in support, "Yes, freedom has made us pay a huge price." He said and hurriedly retreated.

He returned back with a basket filled with sweets and distributed them among his relatives. He was disturbed yet he remained composed.

One of them asked "Have you thought of any name for your infant?"

"Name him lallan, lalla, bhura" and flurry of Indian medieval names came up as a suggestion.

Kisna replied in an instant, "As it is the flavor of the moment I'll name him Swaraj".

'Swaraj' the name sounded alien to them, as if from some another planet.

So another enquired, "What does Swaraj mean?"

"Independence, freedom: freedom from exploitation, freedom from slavery, freedom to live in our own country as a free man and enjoy all the rights of a free man."

"Will Swaraj make a change to our future?" was a somewhat genuine question raised from among the gathering.

Kisna looked down and thought deeply for a moment "I hope so but to me it would be nothing except for a change of guard from white skinned gora sahibs to brown skinned babus." As if he foresighted India's future.

His relatives were village bumpkins. They knew they were free from British Raj, but they didn't know what difference it will make to their lives. Neither did they want to know, nor did they care. They listened half-heartedly some nodded, just for the sake of it and some stared without comprehending anything.

Someone shouted "chalo, chalo baaja bajao" and they returned to what they knew best 'Dance'.

'Sometimes it is good to be dumb wit it makes you ignorant of worldly matters' thought Kisna to himself.

*****

With a tinge of excitement Kisna experienced some anguish. The hushed silence of the village had suddenly come to life. There was chaos everywhere. The flames and fire of Partition finally found its way to his village.

Muslim villagers were running hither–thither, panic stricken gathering anything and everything they can lay their hands on and leaving hurriedly towards their newly carved homeland.

Shambu reached Banne Nawab's place.

Banne Nawab was a heavily built man with thick moustaches that curled upwards. He always wore silk pathani suits. He had a lush green and a huge courtyard where he would splurge on the charpoy and smoke his hookah; he would carry out his own court and dispense judgement. He behaved like a spoilt prince and was always surrounded by four or five servants attentive in his service, catering to all his needs. Banne's forefathers were under high positions under mughal rule and being a progeny of royal blood the benefits had tapered down to him. He had inherited vast acres of land and his residence stood like an imposing palace in this tiny village.

Most of the villagers including Kisna and Anwar Miyan had mortgaged their lands to Banne. He was a tyrant who terrorized the villagers. His decision was final in any village matter and no one could go against his wishes.

Shambu came in with the news, he would fret and tremble whenever he carried bad news, but today's news elated Shambu from within and he was sure that this news will devastate Banne. He had spunk in his voice but he concealed his enthusiasm of permanent riddance from Banne. He disguised his voice in empathy, "Huzoor, leave without delay or you all will slay" saying so he explained the scary ground reality till the last graphic detail.

Banne on hearing the tales for once wetted in his salwar. His stature and imposition went for a toss. He would have as usual slapped Shambu for greeting him with such bad news (even though it was not of his making). But he realized that this issue was much larger and out of even his control.

Fearing for his safety and life, he made up his mind to round up his bedding. He silently conceded defeat to his fate and decided that for his safety the best thing was to migrate. He held his head in his hands in disbelief and mumbled, "Never in my wildest of dreams had I thought of enduring such a tragedy. I'll have to start from a scratch; my all is lost in a sweep." He lamented on his sorrow and left.

He left behind all immovable property and things that could not be transported or were feasible to be carried along. He also left the land papers on which he had taken the thumb impression of villagers. Through the power of these papers he had held the villagers servile and held them by the scruff of their neck. Overnight these treasured papers turned into scrap.

His property was the cynosure of all eyes. Villagers were baying for his blood, waiting for an excuse to pounce and annihilate him, so Banne Nawab through his contacts called for an additional security and arranged for a secret getaway to find a safe passage to his new country.

Now that he was gone, the villagers had a free hand to go on a rampage, but before anything could be ransacked the police platoon from nearby city arrived with sepoys on horses and batons, marching into the village, taking control of law and order and sealing all desolated properties.

The local government was aware of Banne Nawab's iron grip and his relations with the villagers. They in good fate confiscated all the documents into their custody, fearing that they could be robbed, set to flames, shred to bits or could be used to lay bogus or counter claims. They wanted to handover them to their rightful owners once everything calmed down, in due process by sealing the documents, they sealed the fate of villagers land.

***

Their nemesis gone and some Muslim families voluntarily joining the exodus, the village council called for an urgent meeting, the very next day to discuss on the present scenario.

The village council assembled under a huge banyan tree.

Kisna was the youngest member of the council, among the oldies, but by far the most practical. He was an outstanding orator and the council would always take heed of what he said. When he spoke everybody listened and obeyed.

The elders of the council had settled themselves on the platform made of bricks and stones, under the tree, facing the villagers. Anwar Miyan with some of the remaining members of Muslim families sat on one side. Some families had already left, some were adamant to leave whatever be the outcome of the meeting, thereby thinning the Muslim presence as next to nothing, whereas some like Anwar Miyan, who never wanted to leave the village, attended the meeting with a ray of hope.

The huge tree had demarcated area. On the left side sat the guilty or defending party on the right side sat the accusing party. This matter had no particular party defined as accuser or accused but the changed complexities had rendered Muslims as accused and so they by their own choice took left side.

The council members had their say and then it was Kisna's turn. Moving his head across the seated villagers to gain their attention, he spread his hands out and spoke.

"We look the same, have same colored skin, sow the same land, share the same river, face and fight same problems."

To elucidate his speech, he called Anwar Miyan forward. He held his lungi with a pinch and with the other picked up his dhoti and said jokingly, "See, we wear similar clothes, a loose garment below our waist and not the patloon like sahib do".

He waved his hands at the crowd and said, "We eat with our hands and not with spoons and forks and not in ritzy style (he imitated their table manners showing stiffness and snobbery) but by showing gratitude to food by having it humbly, sitting on the ground. One more thing that we share is similar food habits and not bread, butter, cheese."

Someone quickly added, "Toast."

Someone cried from afar, "Biscuits."

He exclaimed, "Yes and things like that". He knew that people had begun to understand his point. He continued, "We have always lived in harmony. There is no bad blood or animosity among us. Skirmishes or any serious rivalry issues are solved by this council.

13

If we go back in history, the Mughals and British they both came, they both plundered, they both conquered, but Mughals made India their home accepted and amalgamated into its culture. We even speak mutually intelligible (milti-julti) language.

He smiled at his own intelligence and said, "Look there is one more similarity" continued "Urdu is the fusion of Persian and Hindi. Have you ever heard British speaking our language if not out of compulsion? They foisted upon us their language but never accepted our language. Today's Muslims are the descendents of Mughals or converts amongst us. They are our very own people. Whereas British are going back sowing the seeds of 'Divide and Rule' the mammoth they created to ensure their survival."

"We have more in common, they pray to different god and we have our own gods, does this one difference make us so different that we can't see an eye to eye."

The voice of dissent rose from one side, "Let them leave, not all but few want to stay then why embrace them in our fold and they now have their own country as per their wish."

Kisna had geared himself for the offensive he gestured towards Anwar Miyan and questioned, "Did he personally ask for a new nation?"

There was temporary silence.

"If he wishes to stay let him stay; put yourself in his shoes and think how deeply forced migration will affect you."

"They are also pushing our people from their lands, why do we play saints?"

"Does two wrongs make a right" He self answered "No".

"If all could be so accommodating there would never be any strife or dispute."

"Wasn't Banne the bloodsucker? All Muslims are bloodsuckers."

"So what, in some other village, some other Hindu Thakur would be doing the same. It is the person that is wrong, never the faith. We should set an example. We should be an exception."

Taking a huge sigh, Kisna continued.

"I am against partition. I cannot prevent that from happening, what I can prevent is the migration of Muslims of my village. I believe in brotherhood. We can't live without each other. My final opinion is we should provide protection and assurance to them. I hope so that I have brought home the point. The rest is with the council to decide." Said Kisna and ended his speech.

The air had become heavy. The crowd began to whisper, there were hushed discussions, squirming, nodding and shaking of heads. A humming sound of human voices filled the air. Kisna's speech had impacted the council's decision, they disregarded the opposition and after thorough discussions they overwhelmingly accepted his plea and stamped on the mandate their approval on support and safety to Muslims.

Good sense prevailed and the damage was minimized. Kisna personally convinced some to stay back and succeeded.

2

❄

After the dust of partition settled, every other village had the same problem of seized documents, sealed homes, desolated properties and farms and many partition related problems to be solved.

An announcer circled village lanes to announce that the newly-formed Indian government have started the procedure of handing back the documents that had been confiscated from the landlord and anyone who had any stake should visit city office.

A group of villages were joined under an officer's undertaking; an office was set up in the city, some twenty kilometers away. Since there were no quick transport facilities, even such a travel was considered a fair distance. The villagers carried out their bullock carts with six to eight persons huddled together like a cattle.

It was soon after rains the gravel path had turned greasy and was covered with puddles of water. The wheel of the cart would often get stuck in the water filled slop and it would call for an extra effort and consumed lot of time to get the bullock cart back on track.

During travel, time seemed to cease. The bullocks pulling the jingling cart and wheels creaking under the pressure of human weight piled up on it were the only sound. To break the stillness villagers would sing folk songs which gradually from swarm of sound would turn into boisterous eruption of high pitched voices with child-like enthusiasm.

But after an initial euphoria waning, weary of singing and abundant time at their disposal they would engage in talks about anything under the sun, even on mundane, odd, frivolous and insane of topics. They would be summoned abruptly any day, so they had to traverse frequently.

They had made many such journeys and on each occasion Anwar Miyan deliberately sat beside Kisna. After they had their solitary meeting at sweet meat mart and with the passing of subsequent chain of events, Anwar Miyan and Kisna shared the relationship of gratitude. Anwar Miyan was grateful for Kisna's sense filled speech at the council meeting and his personal intervention that had helped him change his plan of migration. Whereas Kisna admired Anwar Miyan's love for his country and had became endeared to him for honoring his words. They both influenced each other their friendship grew and they bonded well together.

Meanwhile the wagons in single files plodded slowly and steadily to their destination.

Passing through the corridors of the city on their way to the office, the city displayed the evidence of the recent communal violence, the horrors that remained in the form of burnt houses, haunted streets. And the influx that had followed with refugee camps set up everywhere where pain of refugees, moans of physical scars, wailing for loss of lives, shrieks of infants could be heard. Lost children, young girls abducted and many untold stories could be read on the face of the survivors.

The infrastructure was in shambles, so a playground was converted into a large canopy and divided into tent like offices from within. A make-shift tent was further divided with curtains into two sections, one as a waiting area and the other as an office. The peon would call out on one name at a time into the Babu's office, while others waited patiently or in some cases impatiently idling away their time, waiting for their turn.

The village and small town people addressed an officer as Babu and coincidentally the officer's name was Babulal or simply Babu.

Babulal was a short, bespectacled man in his late twenties. He had a mature face, thick moustache, darkish complexion and was wearing a starched checkered cotton shirt with a row of pens neatly tucked into the pocket, and loose pants. His shoes had been highly polished. Despite being diminutive he made his presence felt, imperiousness perhaps due to the power of his position.

When it was Kisna's turn, the officer with a wry smile welcomed him. Kisna folded his hand in greetings and the officer reading his name on the file asked in a husky voice, "Are you a Brahmin?"

Kisna politely replied, "Yes."

Babu had a grudge against all upper caste people since he belonged to a social class that had always been ostracized and humiliated by them. Now he had the opportunity to get even, a time to repay favors.

"How much land do you own?" he asked bluntly.

"Ten acres" Kisna replied.

He had been standing all the while with folded hands and down cast eyes; the Babu didn't even offers Kisna a seat while he deliberately flicked through the pages in the file.

With a slight whiff of air the curtains would flutter giving the villagers sitting on one side a split second glimpse of what was happening on the other side.

As they were returning home, one villager asked, "Why were you standing with folded hands in front of Babu? He is one of us and not a Sahib."

Kisna explained "Agreed, he is the same as us but he has authority and power to command respect."

No one was yet aware of Babu's social class until another villager broke them the news.

The villager had recognized the young officer as the Dalit boy from his maternal grand-mother's village. Everyone else were shocked, Kisna was surprised and the one who had posted the question regarding folding of hands was out of his wits as he was against stooping even for a fellow Indian and here it was worse still to condescend before a person who was well below their caste. It was like rubbing salt on a wound.

The person who knew his history started his brief biography of how a socially inferior boy had made it big. He said, "Look, this Babulal was a child when his father used to work for Sahib. He would do scavenging at his place and used to take his young son along when he went to work. Babulal would sit in the corner and observe Sahib talking to his family. He was a child prodigy and picked up English language. He would stammer or mouth some broken words. His accent was perfect. The Sahib was impressed with his talent and took him under his tutelage. He went on to become a master in studies. He was intelligent who studied hard to make up for those lost years of deprivation. His proficiency in the Queen's English made easy for him to get selected as an officer.

In my childhood I would see that if they happen to pass by the path that we were taking, he and his father would rush aside to stand at further than an arm's length with downcast eyes mindful that even their shadows should not fall on us. His father would be bare-chested with coir rope tied to his waist and broom dangling on his back like a donkey's tail.

The one who ate our leftovers is now dancing on our heads. As if one Sahib gone doing all the damage was not enough that now we have another to aggravate our pride." saying so he spat indignantly.

"Don't be mean, can't you see talent pays" Kisna interrupted.

But the other villagers didn't agree with Kisna's opinion they ignored him and continued to argue, "Why didn't the upper caste people in his village object? Why did they allow a cleaner's son to get hold of Saraswati?"

"All this happened in secrecy. The Sahib knew the caste hierarchy that existed in India and he very well knew that if the people would know they would resent. So every day as usual his father took him along and no one doubted anything unusual and by the time anybody got the air of it, it was too late. Sahib came forward in his defense and no one had the stomach to dare the Sahib's decision" the villager replied.

One old upper caste villager had all his life lived by the principle of caste discrimination held close to his heart found it tough to digest the revelation. He fumed and growled, "What are you saying? I will forgo my land but would not budge in front of him henceforth. He had made me impure."

The others too agreed to his viewpoint, but didn't bluster about forgoing their lands as the stakes were too high.

Kisna disregarded caste system and shook his head in disapproval. He reasoned, "It's not his fault that he is born a Dalit. He is human like us. We have created these caste barriers. It is us who have deemed people as superior or inferior".

His words ignited rancor, "Stop your lecturing us every now and then. Last time we supported your anti-partition and saving Muslim cause as that was on humanitarian grounds but this is a matter of religious beliefs, you dare do not teach us religion."

"As you know the facts from now on you should feel ashamed to deign in front of him, your forefathers will never forgive you. You are a Brahmin and don't you feel defiled? It's my humble plea that next time you stand upright and not hunch-backed."

Kisna's words fell on deaf ears as everybody shrugged their shoulders and sneered. They were of collective opinion that karma decided their position and to be born in a class was predestined and deserving and thus the perpetual shackles should not be broken or tempered with. Kisna was left isolated and Anwar Miyan understandably stood mute and neutral while others parted away to show their disapproval and protest to what they termed were his illogical views. The day indeed ended with heated arguments.

As they reached back to the village the rift of caste system appeared putative with dhobi, mali, sutar, sen, khumbhar, mochi, chamar and many more each forming their own clusters.

The next time they went to the city, the old villager who had gone wild on the argument over caste did not accompany them.

Kisna thought, "Gashes of caste system has penetrated so deep into Indian culture that it will take a long time to change people's perceptions."

The villagers made regular trips to the city in the hope that their problems would finally be adhered to. But it was not to be as the questions would change, the result would be same. It became a daily pattern.

Finally one day, frustrated by repetitive questioning one of the villager dashed forward to confront Babu, "Why is there so much of dilly-dallying? Why are we not getting what is rightfully ours?" The others tried to restrain and pacify him.

On their way back Kisna hopped into the wagon of the rebellious villager as he was a member of another wagon. Kisna cooled him down, he said "Relax, get the anger out of your system. This will soon become the norm. You develop a thick skin and brace yourself, for the worst is yet to follow. This may be the first instance of harassment but is certainly not going to be the last. This is called 'Red-Tapism.'

All asked at once "What the hell is it?"

"Red-Tapism is the tactic the Babus apply to give them ample time to negotiate."

"Negotiate about what" they asked in chorus.

"Commission" said Kisna and explained "It's the illegal income they earn over and above their salaries by taking money under the table".

"That's unfair. We were better off under the Raj; at least there was no corruption."

"Yes, because everyone over their work for the benefit of queen of their country, with their sole purpose of filling the coffers of the majesty."

"So does that mean we Indians are less patriotic?"

"Patriotism for us works in concerns, first we are concerned towards our children, then towards the queen of our hearts and then towards our country, our patriotism passes through many filters and for them their definition of Patriotism works in reverse order, for them their country comes first. But it is too early to make value judgment. Let time pass."

This is how another day passed and so did many.

Then one day, Babu called Kisna into his office. The bureaucrat has a sharp eye, and through his repeated questioning he had summed up Kisna's intelligent quotient, he had found his voice that could act as his emissary and ferry his words around.

He brought his voice down to a whisper and said discreetly, "Sign me two acres of your land and get back eight acres without further delay. Decide fast or else will keep circling endlessly. If you agree to my proposal pass on my message to your fellow villagers. Cash or kind anything will do." He winked and smiled cunningly.

Kisna was intelligent, he got the gist of Babu's offer, he was waiting for the ice to break and now it finally had.

He was in dire financial straits and had only way out. It was a god send opportunity. He thought this was not a bad offer; he under zamindar's rule would never have been able to repay his entire loan and though being the owner would still be landless, now he had the opportunity to claim his land and be the real owner with registered land under his name. He readily agreed.

In the course of this negotiation he learned the new system of governance and Babudom and of days to come.

He explained the strategy to the others and convinced them to do as Babu had suggested. He too was parting with his piece of land in order to gain the remaining part, and it was the only way to get their land back without getting caught in bureaucratic hassles.

Kisna was like a one eyed leader among the blind. Everybody blindly followed and got their land back.

At last their agonizing wait ended.

3

⁂

Kisna now had eight acres of land, in the past, whatever he had produced was divided into two parts, of which one had to be given to landlord as interest on the mortgage he had taken. The other was not enough to survive for the rest of the year. The situation would worsen in the years when there would be little or no rain, because no matter what the circumstances were, the quantity he had to give to the landlord would remain the same.

Kisna though with a discounted piece of land was contended; he devoted all his time to farming, and through sheer hard work he had transformed his barren land into fertile farmland. Forgoing two acres was not at all a bad option.

Three years passed by and in the year 1950. Kisna became father again. He had another son whom he named Sandeep.

Agriculture is dependent on the monsoon. It's unfailingly for rains year after year. Monsoon plays tricks with the spirit of India, brings blessings of plenty or sorrow of scanty. Either way the dice falls, villages and its inhabitants are at its mercy.

Excessive rain ravages the villages, the river bulges and breaks embankments, they gurgle and swirl, overflow and flood farmlands, sway recklessly and carry with it crops and corpses, rocks and stones, dead cattle and fodder, home and shelter, lives and livelihood and when its fury recedes, it deposits the debris in the fold of the seas and lay bare the devastation.

Scarce rainfall has its own share of woes. It brings with it drought, famine, wilted crops and thirsty land.

Unpredictable rainfall means an uncertain future. If not floods, drought play spoilsport.

North India was facing severe drought conditions the year Sandeep was born.

Even the indefatigable Kisna could not coax his fields to produce any crops. The wells had dried up; the cracks had started to appear in the parched land. The soil even when dug deep had no traces of moisture. There remained not a drop of water.

Giving up all hope, Kisna went to live in the city for two years. There he took on sundry jobs such as carrying luggage, pulling carts, running errands. He worked very hard but was poorly paid and made to slog for too little and then whatever he saved, he sent back home, but even that was not enough to make two ends meet. He felt short changed.

Kisna returned to the village with immediate effect when the drought conditions eased. Being a simple man he couldn't adjust with the corrupt and fast life in the city.

He felt homesick and longed for the warmth of village life. He was a village man to the core. He vowed never to stay in the city again.

***

India was reviving herself after Independence. The government had adapted a populist agenda and had initiated many welfare schemes, such as providing fertilizers and seeds at subsidized rates, giving land to landless farmers and encouraging unskilled laborers to work in the fields. They had also launched irrigation projects whereby the government would build water storage tanks, tube wells, pipelines connected to water reservoirs, canals and provide all the required agricultural tools in public private partnership. The condition they proposed was that the government would pitch in with half of the cost and each farmer would bear the other half.

Kisna saw a bright future in this project but did not have the finances.

It was the year 1952; Babulal was now head of the irrigation department. The past five years had been good for him. He had received regular promotions, not because he was good at his job, but because he had accustomed to the way the government machinery worked, he circumvented the situation and cleverly used the underprivileged card to his advantage.

The seeds of corruption that had been sowed with the departure of British were now flourishing, its venom spreading its tentacles to all departments of governments.

Near the building's entrance, Kisna encountered many shady looking men approaching him to get his work done effortlessly and in no time. Kisna instinctively shrugged them aside in a bid to himself do the needful. When he reached the office, he was unaware of what was in store, he was in for a rude shock, that his and Babulal's path would cross again. Babulal too, was taken aback for a moment, he signaled him to take a seat, sifted through his file, smiled his cunning smile and understanding his needs came to the point at once.

"Sell me some of your land and I'll forward your documents steadfastly" then continued, "If not, then meet a man outside the office premises. He would be wearing a black pant and white half sleeved shirt; black shoes and white wrist band wrist watch; black belt with white buckle; white hat with black strip, a contrast of black and white. Can't help our system work in black and white" He jiggled in his chair laughing nastily.

"He is working on my behalf as I can't go on asking straightforwardly. I know you and so I directly kept the proposal. If you go and get the work done through him, either way it will come back to me. He will take his and I'll take my cut. You'll end up paying two times for single service, now you decide if you want the short cut."

To make the file to move the desks, it has to be lubricated and aware of how things worked. Kisna without wasting any time or without wasting any efforts, sidelining the assistance of bottlenecks and even though fully aware that he was the partaker in breaking the law, he thought, 'If I part with two acres. I'll still be left with six acres enough to sustain my family and as monsoon is approaching I would be able to make good the expenses incurred.'

So he accepted the offer in a single meeting and when he was leaving Babulal's office, Babulal gave him a parting advice, "If you ever feel the need to sell your land don't go around searching for buyers, my door are always open. You are after all an intelligent person sans my input." He chuckled.

So Kisna sold his two acres to reap the benefits of the irrigation facilities.

The monsoon was good that year and his efforts were rewarded handsomely.

The next year Kisna again became a father for the third time. Swaraj and Sandeep now had the company of a sister.

But then tragedy struck. The lack of proper medical facilities led to some post delivery complications resulting in his wife's death.

Kisna was grief stricken but he put up a brave front in face of adversity, picked himself up and moved on with his life. He was now saddled with the responsibility of taking care of three children on his own.

Swaraj began to go to school. The school was in a fenced-off government land. With no school building there was a single one room cottage partitioned into two; one as a principal's cabin and another stocked with minimal stationery, furniture and facilities.

Solitary chairs were placed under each of the large trees-mango, neem, banyan or tamarind in the compound. The black cloth boards were hung from the trunks of the trees. Group of children sat over laid out mats under the trees, each tree denoted a standard. There was no stationery, no uniform, no classrooms, no attendance register and no furniture. The teachers were underpaid and lackadaisical and so were few desultory students, but it still classified as a school.

If government lacked resolve and resource for imparting education, the villagers showed apathy for gaining education. Education for them hung on the last rung of their priorities. For them, children meant, the more the merrier, more hands at work and the more sources of income. They were unconcerned about illiteracy, unemployment or adding to the burden of the nation's limited resources.

Kisna would campaign from door to door, telling the villagers about the benefits of education and persuading them to send their children to school. They relented but half-heartedly.

The children would come to school half-asleep, wearing unwashed clothes, their hair frizzy and uncombed and with running noses that they would wipe with the edge of their shirts. They were more interested in playing then studying.

Swaraj though came to school looking clean and smart, thanks to the pains his father took to get him dressed for school.

Swaraj was six years old. He matured too quickly for a six year child. He would take care of Sandeep and Nirmala like a mother. Years passed by Swaraj grew and so did everybody around him. By limited means the three brothers and sisters got educated in village school.

Swaraj on his first day to school met Siraj and they became best buddies from day one. Siraj was Anwar

Miyan's son. By the time Sandeep was old enough to go to school Siraj got stuck to Swaraj like glue. Siraj had cemented his friendship with Swaraj, they had become inseparable. Siraj always had something praiseworthy to be told about Swaraj. He prided himself in lauding Swaraj. Siraj was genuine in his praise for Swaraj, but Sandeep felt he did it on purpose. He never left two brothers alone.

Swaraj and Siraj grew closer and as closer they grew Sandeep drifted further apart.

After school hours Swaraj Siraj and Sandeep would walk back home together passing muddy lanes, green fields, crossing the river bed and playing childish games like throwing pebbles and broken tree branches into the river.

Sandeep had the trait of being inquisitive. He after watching for a while noticed the regularity with which the pebbles sank but branches stayed afloat, "What is the mystery behind this?" He asked Swaraj.

"Stones are heavier and have a greater density than water and so they sank, whereas branches have lower mass density and are lighter, thus they float."

Sandeep made a mental note of what he had learnt.

During sultry summer days the trio would toss their clothes aside on the river bank and spend hours splashing and swimming. They would have swimming competitions that Sandeep would win hands down.

Always winning, Sandeep one day ran home to tell Kisna, in a manner to impress, that he had yet again won the race. Kisna dryly said, "Thank Swaraj, for he taught you how to swim."

Sandeep felt snubbed at Kisna's cold shouldered response, killing the joy out of his win. He sulked thinking 'Why should Swaraj take credit for my achievement?'

On other occasion Sandeep and Swaraj jointly decided to steal mangoes for fun. They trespassed into some villager's field and Sandeep climbed the tree while Swaraj stood their guarding and gathering. The owner of the farm saw from afar that Sandeep was perched on the tree, plucking the mangoes. He ran with his stick towards him but when he reached near he saw Swaraj. He mellowed down instantly. The villager was a known man to them. He knew Swaraj as a decent child and Sandeep as mischievous. So he chided Swaraj but reprimanded Sandeep by wringing his ears.

Sandeep was appalled at his double standards. He began to nurture a feeling of grudge for Swaraj, for his sugar coated nature, for his benign smile, for his innocent face and for his gaining undue favoritism. He felt as if Swaraj was milk-washed and he was a devil.

Every time Sandeep played any prank or did any mischief or was complained by anyone. Swaraj like a big daddy would teach Sandeep manners. Sandeep felt Swaraj was behaving too big for his boots.

At annual felicitation function held in school when Swaraj was awarded for his outstanding overall performance, Sandeep observed from the corner of his eyes a twinkle of admiration and glow of pride in Kisna. Sandeep felt neglected.

Villager's attitude, Siraj's purloining his relation and Kisna's predilection impacted the infantile mind of

Sandeep. With time his dislike for Swaraj became profound. He considered Swaraj as his competitor and decided to move ahead of him at any cost, by hook or by crook.

One day Sandeep teased a pack of dogs and they chased him. He was scared and ran away fast; overtaking, Swaraj and Siraj who were walking at a little distance ahead of him.

When Swaraj saw what was happening he somehow hurled himself out of the harm's way while Siraj pelted stones to chase the dogs away.

Sandeep sprinted away without worrying about Swaraj's safety. He knew that Siraj would definitely complain about him to Kisna so he ran straight towards his farm and hid himself behind the tree nearer to hearing distance of Kisna.

Siraj was angry by Sandeep's unconcern; he narrated this incident to Kisna secretly hoping that he would admonish Sandeep. And Siraj had rightly thought so because Swaraj had always rescued Sandeep from deep troubles. But Kisna held his son close and told Siraj "Listen, my two sons are equal to me like my two eyes but in character both are complete opposite. He moved his finger up down and said "North-South."

"If Swaraj is an altruist, intelligent, wise, industrious, considerate, benevolent and responsible" Kisna stopped waving his hands in dismissal.

"When Sandeep does not come to the farm to help me, your dear friend takes his side and says that he is here to help, why worry about Sandeep, let him study. I know he pretends to study; he is a lazy ass. The total opposite of Swaraj" He sighed.

Kisna wanted to avoid Sandeep's character assassination. How could he not? After all Sandeep was his own flesh and blood.

But it was a fact Sandeep was selfish, shrewd, cunning, sly, slothful; opportunistic and his most potent weapons were his silence and stealth.

Hearing Kisna, Sandeep construed the meaning of North-South, total opposite, lazy ass but skipped the phrase where he said that 'My two sons are equal to me like my two eyes'.

***

In the course of ten years, the small school had grown considerably from a primary school to a tenth grade school by adding a higher standard every some years to its tally to achieve the distinction of being an only matriculation school in the village. Apart from that nothing much had changed.

Swaraj was now sixteen years old, a teenager on the advent of adulthood. Yet, he still retained his boyish innocence and charm, despite the faint traces of moustache on his upper lips and a gruffish voice.

Sandeep had also entered his teens, but there was no marked distinction visible in his appearance.

Siraj was taller, healthier and looked more mature than his age, perhaps this was because of his luxuriant facial hair.

Swaraj was now old enough to earn a living. Bombay was a big name in the village. Every young man dreamt of going there to work and make a fortune.

The 'Gateway of India' welcomed foreigners to its shore. But for the rural population it was 'Gateway to success'.

It meant the same for Swaraj.

Finally Kisna called Swaraj and told him, "You are old enough now. Boys of your age have moved to the cities to work. I have your brother and sister to look after. Our village school is till matriculation. I do not have the capacity to send you to city for further studies. Education open many doors but the key to it is money and my key has abraded. My earnings are not enough to take care of all of us. I know you love studying, but you are the eldest, the only one capable of sacrifice. I am bound by circumstances. Can you suggest any way out of this conundrum?"

Swaraj knew his father's predicament. Even before Kisna asked him for his opinion, he had prepared himself for it; if and when the situation arose. He had discussed this with Siraj some time ago.

"I want to go to Bombay so that I can help you out. Siraj is accompanying me."

Getting Siraj's family to agree was a cakewalk. Anwar Miyan held the highest regard for Kisna, he still was indebted to him for his intervention that had helped him stay back and just the mention of Swaraj name as a companion was enough for him to grant his permission.

Moreover, Siraj's family's problems were not very different from Kisna's. They too wanted him to go to Bombay.

4

Swaraj and Siraj set off on their journey to Bombay, the city of dreams.

Both were unskilled, naïve novices, but had some acquaintances who worked at Bombay port.

"My, my, the city of dreams is a damn good dream." They both collectively gasped.

They saw before them a vibrant new world- tall buildings, countless people, sea that stretched far into the horizon- so very different from their dusty, pathetically slow, dull village.

At the port they saw for the first time people from other countries like Europe, America, the Middle East, the foreigners that came in the ships that docked here.

The dock had been constructed during British rule. The port walls had been fortified with heavy stone; the floor had been paved with flagstones. Its surface covered with moss and besmeared by tidal waves had turned dark bottle green, making it slippery.

There were several ticket counters, sheltered with awnings, wooden benches for travelers, a fish market, stalls selling travel wares and snacks.

At one end there was a multistory building that housed the offices overseeing the port affairs. One such office was the manager's cabin. He had been designated by government to look after the porters affairs which included keeping records of the number of porters required, allocating uniforms, badge numbers, organizing medical check-ups to ensure that they were fit enough to do strenuous work, arranging their accommodation and mess food, as well as addressing their grievances. The lost and found department was also located here. The porters would collect the luggage that had been misplaced, unclaimed or forgotten and would deposit them here.

Only recognized licensed porters were allowed entry into the port. They were distinguished by their uniforms that consisted of a blue shirt, beige trousers, and a buckled belt with their badge number engraved on the buckle and a towel. The towel was either tied around the waist like a belt or draped around the neck like a dupatta or loosely fastened as a turban. They were also provided with a long coiled rope that was used to fasten two or three bags.

Their boss the manager was a young man, anyone who wanted to work in the port had to be approved by him. His educational qualification was basic, just about what was required for the job. He was practical and took quick decisions, but he was always fair. However he had one strange quirk, he was whimsical and took instant likes or dislikes to people when he first met them. To gain his favors a person had to be in his good books. Fortunately he took a liking to Swaraj and Siraj from day one.

Swaraj and Siraj soon discovered that co-workers were like a family away from home. They met many interesting characters, many of whom had nicknames that reflected their particular personality trait. For example one was called

'Pheku' because he always spun tall tales,

'Nawab' as he affiliated his ancestry to Nawab of Lucknow. He claimed that his forefathers were the Nawab eons ago and would reminiscence about his glorious past as told to him through generations. His companions teasingly called him Nawab ki aulad which got shortened to Nawab.

Another one was called 'Tiger', who had boasted that his uncles once tamed a tigress and when he was born he was fed on her milk, so he was a tiger! But he was a moron and thought that everyone had his nonsensical talk.

In such an environment how could Swaraj and Siraj remain aloof from this naming game? They too got their names according to their peculiarity.

Siraj was called Dyna Hath (Right Hand) because he always seconded Swaraj's opinion, advice, suggestion and idea. He was like his echo, almost as if he was a henchmen to a don, a sidekick to a hero.

Swaraj was nicknamed 'Mukhiya' since he was always there to solve their problems. His advices were philosophical, and he was always ready to pontificate on any subject. What he said was precise and thought-provoking but it was considered as boring and dull particularly since his audiences were poor illiterate souls who found it hard to decipher the context of his explanations. Maybe he had it in his genes. Kisna was knowledgeable and all conclusive, so was Swaraj.

And so the five of them Pheku, Tiger, Nawab, Swaraj and Siraj formed a group of friends who like the other such groups would crouch in huddle together, chatting during the breaks.

Swaraj and Siraj soon adapted to the new city and their place of work.

The inner world of the port was rarely seen by the outside world. They were in total one hundred and twenty porters working at the port but at any given time, only eighty porters would be working on regular basis as some would be on personal leave, some would be ill, some gone to their villages. Their affairs were handled by the manager.

After the British had left, the new earned freedom was interpreted and implemented by Indians in the way they pleased.

The port was the vital link for international trade. In the early days of Independence, India was a closed economy in revival phase, Imports of several items such as branded wrist watches, cosmetics, foreign liquor, electronics, gold etc, were banned. However this did not affect the cream class, the privileged and the connoisseur of brands, they had access to these luxury goods as long as they were willing to pay the price.

Such contraband items were smuggled on the dhows of fisherman and private contractors. Thus to facilitate its distribution, there was a black market that only dealt with smuggled goods. There was never a dearth of market but very few daredevils to satiate their demands.

One such smuggler was a young Pathan called 'Salim Pasha'. His family had discarded him because of his radical views. He had dreams of conquering the world glittering in his eyes. He was full of youthful abandon. There was a vacant slot and an untapped market to be ruled. It was without a clear cut leader but had small syndicates working independently. There was a need to organize the network. He with his enterprising confidence eyed the potential and took the lead. He soon turned into a self-made terror.

The long costal line was still pristine and there were large swatches of land that remained deserted, through which there was always a possibility of being spotted and captured. This was where Salim Pasha entered the scene. He had slowly started to encroach upon the empty land outside the port by putting up a few temporary shelters made with bamboo and tarpaulin sheets. These shacks grew into blocks of houses and very soon the houses had multiplied and grown into a sprawling slum that had become so dense that it obscured the port activities.

The slum had its own gas, water and electricity connections and its inhabitants had been issued ration cards, giving a stamp of legality. These advantages gave it solidity which made it difficult for the authorities to demolish the structures.

From being a small time smuggler, Salim had become the undisputed owner of this wide tract of land. He was now a slum lord, messiah; provider of shelter to the homeless and needy, the don of his little fiefdom. He was respected and venerated by his followers who considered him to be like Robin Hood. But his rivals, the police and the system dreaded him.

The slum had become an eyesore along the beautiful promenade the British had built; its shanties stretching as far as the eyes could see. Swarthy children and fisher-folk swam and splashed in waters that had been polluted by the slush and sewage flowing from the colony.

It had become a menace for vigilance for the port authorities. To ensure security they had built a high wall along its perimeter and placed tetra pod shaped boulders in the sea to somewhat beautify the squalid image of the sea shore.

But in a few months, the wall had been breached and the slum dwellers used the hole as a passageway from the colony to the shore. Slum couples longing privacy, early morning defectors exposing their shame, eunuchs, urchins, drunkards, anti social elements all made the sea shore their playing fields. The space between the boulders was used as a dumping ground for garbage and debris, further desecrating the beauty of the environment.

At election time Salim Pasha was a much sought after and courted by politicians as he held sway over the area and the people he controlled. The political parties saw his landscape bearers as vote bank. He would wear spick and span clothes to match his wear with political sobriety that gave him certain gravitas. He would ferry the politicians around the area urging people to vote for them.

The politicians made rounds to the slums wearing their plastic, pasted and practiced smile and literally begged for votes, knowing very well that these were merely ploys to win elections and those acting smart could be screwed after election.

Life was flourishing in the fast lane of crime.

Until one day it hit a speed breaker. Until one day the inevitable happened.

On one routine political entourage with drummers, loudspeakers, flags, banners, hooting, shouting, sloganeering and with crowd of onlookers, passing within the by-lanes of slums, Salim's eyes fell on a girl and he lost his heart in an instant.

Her facial features were chiseled to perfection. Her fair complexion was her gift of Kashmiri lineage; gold trinket dangled elegantly in her slender pierced ear lobes, a diamond in the nose-ring sparkled in the sunshine. Her salwar-kameez fitted and shaped her body contours immaculately and was protuberant at right places. Her hair textured dark brown and hennaed fell on her shoulder in a wave as she stood on the edge of her room's door watching the posse pass by.

As he passed close-by from her, her flowing strand of hair and her flowing dupatta touched him and he felt as if the freshness of cool breeze had caressed him, her permeating fragrance bedazzled him.

She missed him in the hullabaloo of noises, whereas his heart selected her leaving him with no option for choices.

She looked like an ethereal beauty; a lyrical composition. Her grace could give Bollywood heroine run for their money.

But only, she was a religious, orthodox and a homely Muslim girl.

Salim saw her in the confines of her home, in her home wear, but when in the marketplace or outside her home her garb was a head scarf tightly worn and nicely wrapped covering her pretty face and a loose black cloak draped over her body shielding her decency and modesty.

Conflicting to her tenderness Salim Pasha was a young man fond of dark, flashy, bright and lurid shirts paired with only black elephant-ears bell bottomed pants to go with pointed heeled black shoes. He always left the top two buttons for his shirt undone exposing his hairy chest and holy talisman he wore around his neck. He wore several gold rings, studded with rubies, emeralds, sapphires and other precious stones that he wore for good luck on his fingers that made his hands feel full and heavy; he would play with his fingers by keeping it on the table and drum it on the surface; one look on his pudgy fingers were enough to intimidate the person seated opposite of him. During fights, his rings worked for him like weapon, his punch on the face would leave the imprint of the ring or slash the face with the sharpness of a razor.

His conduct gave him an aura of invincibility. He would linger ideally in the slums some supplicating in adoration and some in fear.

He was rouge, brutish and a reprobate.

Salim had ruled the slums unchallenged for two years, but images of that beautiful girl clouded his thoughts and had made him somewhat gentler. He was longing to see her again. Seated with his group of ruffians he spotted her.

Excited, he drifted like a nugget of iron towards magnet. He went up to her and with his signature hand fingers touching his forehead, he greeted her with a salaam, "O lady can I have a talk with you?"

She knew who he was and was alarmed, she quickly downed her eyes and replied timidly, "Yes."

"I saw you some time ago at one of the rounds regarding election work and since that day you have been in my thoughts for every single day." He caught his breath, closed his eyes and blurted out, "I am in love with you."

She was startled but replied, "And to how many girls have you proposed to in this way mister?"

"I don't need to propose to any other girl; they just come and fall into my lap. You are the first girl, I am proposing to sincerely."

The girl was amazed by his obvious arrogance and effrontery and from her stupefied reaction he too realized how stupid and conceited he had been.

The girl said, "I am a simple, conservative and decent girl from a humble background and you are a Bhai, powerful rouge, we have nothing in common."

He persisted, "You can redeem me. I am willing to change myself for you."

The girl stood still, fazed for a moment then took soft steps backwards and slowly walked away. Salim too didn't expect an urgent reply so he stood his ground till she left.

The girl's family was in a transit. All her father's relative had migrated to a neighboring country, and he too yearned to leave as soon as possible. Days, week, months and now a year or two had passed and their wait was getting longer by the day. The legal work was taking agonizingly long time. However they had kept their reason for stay in the area and hope of migration a tight secret.

Salim, on the other hand, had lost all interest in his activities. He was no longer interested in terrorizing the neighborhood. His terror was fading under his beauty. He was so much in love that he would make several rounds of her house, hoping to catch a glimpse of her. His unrequited love had become the talk of the town further frustrating the girl and her family.

One fine day after a long wait her father brought home the good news that their voyage had been scheduled for early next morning. They decided to leave in the dark of the night, unseen and without saying a word to anyone.

The girl wrote the letter in Urdu to Salim and attached it to the back of the door.

Every time Salim walked past her house he would find the door locked and think that the family had gone somewhere and would return later. Even after some days when there was still no sign of them he broke open the door and found the letter.

'Sorry Bhai,

Everyone call you Bhai out of respect but I am calling you bhai like a brother. I have never had any feelings for you. I would prefer my life partner to be a simple, down to earth, ordinary person who had succeeded because he has struggled and worked hard for it. You do have not a single trait to be the prince of my dreams. By the time you will get this letter, we would be far from your reach, far from you and your slum world. There is no point chasing me. Forget about me. Have a good life. Good bye'.

The letter was like a lightning bolt from nowhere. She had spurned his love and vanished without a trace. His hopes had been deflated, his eyes dilated, his eyes moistened, tears rolled down from the sides of his eyes. His senses hit a road block, his world spun out of control, the floor beneath his legs shifted and his legs felt weak. His anger had reached boiling point and he let out a piercing shriek and collapsed to the floor, bellowing expletives and talking gibberish. His world shattered beyond repair. He had a nervous breakdown and went into a coma.

After years of being in a vegetative state, he gained consciousness but lost sanity. He lost his ability to determine good from bad, true from a lie, prank from seriousness. The sanity to judge the ebb and flow of life was lost on him. From imposing don he turned into innocent child, a child away from the trickery of life, rejoicing in little pleasures; laughing aloud and clapping. He understood gestures but lost reflexes to react. He could shout but his voice lost words. He looked like a lovelorn ascetic roaming the by-lanes of his own slum; lost and forgotten.

By the time he gained consciousness, his grip on the underworld elapsed, his rivals became bold; his friends splintered into groups and formed their own gangs. His evil empire had come crashing down. His legacy as a Bhai was now a clouding memory, overtaken by a new Bhai.

From Bhai he was now teased as 'Yeda Bhai' or 'Majnu Bhai'. His terror had turned into pity, from a roaring tiger he diminished into a meek mewling cat. From a stylish

Salim Pasha he was now a mentally impaired man with grubby face, mucky clothes and always slobbering. His hair locks bushy and a tangled mess, while his manicured fingernails were filled with grime. He looked like a lunatic.

The outer side of the port wall was the concrete jungle beside the sea shore. Likewise of the porter's, every person's life had a story worth a novel. Yet Yeda Bhai's story did struck the chord because he was the one responsible for the presence of slums attached to the port walls, because he though being the creator of the slums was now an unknown entity, because he would stray onto the port premises unhindered daily, because he was a part and parcel of daily entertainment dose to porter's lives, because he was the only one who had unlimited access into port premises and was not shooed away to the other side.

Just before the tragedy, when he was dreaming about his marriage to his lady-love, he would hum songs from the movies. That single thought had lingered with him so now whenever he would hear a marriage song, a romantic song or a hip-hop song; he would dance much to everybody's amusement.

The manager had binoculars to scout on the on-goings from the high end of his window. He was a strict disciplinarian, however tough on the outside he gave some liberties and would join in the fun in free time. He had a transistor in his cabin that operated on electricity as well as battery he would carry it down whenever he would see Yeda Bhai lingering near idle sitting porters. He would turn the volume to the maximum and the show would start. Yeda Bhai would become their source of entertainment.

He would spontaneously swagger into wild unsynchronized dancing on hearing foot tapping music and the porters clapped vigorously to increase the tempo and encourage Yeda to dance with gay abandon.

When it came to spending all of them were thrift by spending minimum and saving maximum. Swaraj was extra cautious he was altruist to the core lived parsimoniously and saved as much as he could so that his brother and sister could study. Siraj was a bit of spend-drift, he splurged on movies, his favorite past time.

The days away from the family passed in the midst of port life, fellow porters and dream city.

5

❄

Four years passed by Sandeep sat for his matriculation exam and to the astonishment of Swaraj and Kisna, he failed.

"Can you imagine such a studious person failing?" Siraj remarked to Swaraj.

When Swaraj heard the news, he felt miserable. Siraj reasoned, "Why are you making such a fuss about it?"

Swaraj replied, "I was good at studies that you know very well, but as an elder brother I had to think about the betterment of my siblings. I dropped out of school because I wanted him to excel in life. I had big dreams for him. But he crashed all my expectations. And the bigger reason for my disappointment is that he has great expectation from Bombay city. He is lured by the name of Bombay. He thinks this is some kind of a magical world with pots of money. And I am saddened by his decision to come to work in this back breaking job. And what will happen when he is touched by reality."

Siraj's response was muted. He knew that Swaraj was practical but he could be a bit sentimental at times there was no vice in him and so he never imagined any vice in others. He believed in karma and blamed destiny for his bad fortune and he was presently in one of his melancholy moods.

Siraj but on the other hand was talkative, quick to dispense advice even in matters he could not comprehend. "Over dependence on destiny is foolish, under dependence is audacious. Believe in it but don't blame destiny for your downfall." He advised somewhat incoherently. He soon forgot about what he said but his words lingered in Swaraj's mind.

Finally Sandeep joined them in Bombay.

***

Sandeep had deliberately failed. He had heard exciting tales about Bombay and he had been bitten by the big city bug. He conjured Bombay to be a fairy tale world. But the real world is so very different from the imagined world. This was the lesson Sandeep learned once he reached Bombay. He faced the reality, understood the struggles of a life in a metro, his air castles decimated into dust.

On Swaraj's recommendation the manager gave him a job at the port. A toilsome job was all Swaraj could offer to Sandeep, which was all he had.

Sandeep had been athletic and active when he was in school, he was of a linear frame and had the power of a village boy, accustomed and capable to carry heavy load on his back or on his shoulder, but as soon as he came to Bombay and saw the strenuous work, his enthusiasm faded and oozed out like the pulp of a fruit. His pace slackened. Sandeep would trudge along like a languorous cow carrying the luggage. Seeing this Swaraj after completing his haul would rush to make amends for his laggardness.

The manager who kept a watch on the happenings on the dock from his cabin window observed Sandeep's slack performance; he observed his deliberate plodding for some days. He called him into his cabin to have a word with him. The manager was crossed with him and berated Sandeep in sternest of words. "Where do you think you are working? This is port and not a garden. You are a porter not a gardener who can spend his time strolling around". The manager reminded Sandeep about the job on his hand.

Sandeep did not respond to his reprimand. Swaraj was worried and so had accompanied Sandeep. Swaraj did all the pleadings and mutterings on behalf of Sandeep "Sir, he is new to the job and will get used to it soon. I will train him, please give him some time".

The manager warned him again. "There are many unemployed people in our country who will grab at the opportunity to work at the port. It is because of your brother's assurance that you are still working at the port. Alter your behavior or leave." The manager didn't even look at Sandeep and with the wave of his hand suggested him to leave.

Sandeep smirked slyly and walked out, unrepentant. Swaraj remained to plead his case, but manager interrupted him by saying, "From what I can judge, your brother is good for nothing fellow and will be a liability for you, so you better be careful."

Swaraj thanked him profusely as if he was the culprit and departed only after being assured that the manager had cooled down.

The manager did not like Swaraj appealing, he held a soft corner and so he ignored Sandeep's laziness as a first time offence.

If in village Sandeep encountered discrimination in favor of Swaraj, the city he felt was no different, here it was co-workers attitude, Siraj's lauding and manager predilection. His position vis-à-vis Swaraj again came to square. The lesser he wanted to hate Swaraj for what he was the more it became intense; he was unable to gather the reason for the reverence that Swaraj earned in other people's eyes. Sandeep other reason for stuffing up of his frustration was his faulty assumption of a better city life.

Here again it was the same garbage and living in dumps condition.

Here again instead of being crossed with himself, he blamed Swaraj that he was caught in this job because Swaraj knew nothing better and he had to be with him, doing the same work.

Here instead of introspecting deep into his own self to find out his faults he cursed Swaraj for gaining the spotlight and ushering him into oblivion.

Altering himself Sandeep set out to explore the city life. He got sucked into the razzmatazz of city life of exhibited whores, of cheap movies, of deliciously lined up food-stalls, of roadside betting. He after all found out the true colors of Bombay, his escape to the life he longed for.

This facet of his life he would live secretly and tactfully and appear deceitfully decent in front of everyone. But even the other workers had figured out Sandeep's attitude and had given him the name that befitted his personality-Girghit, or chameleon.

Both Siraj and the manager had one thing in common, and that was that they were keen judges of a person character. And what was more they both disliked Sandeep.

***

Work at the port was unscheduled. Some days were hectic as hell and some days had no work to tell. The days of leisure were when the staff actually enjoyed themselves.

Bollywood movies would be the hot topic. The men would spend long hours discussing the latest films, they would all day hum the songs, they would get aroused by the show of heroine's cleavage, they drooled over her seductive gyrations, the hero's muscles would fascinate them immensely, the fight sequence and villain bashing would excite them, they would arm wrestle each other and get involved in mock fights, they copied the hero's hairstyle and his dressing style, they discussed the comedy, the tragedy and their acting skills. The movie would be discussed at end until another Friday release that would overshadow the hangover of the previous movie. They all literally lived cinema, getting involved in it as if the box-office depended on their opinions and as if movies were the only get away from their rigorous and boring life.

Swaraj dismissed their conversations as hackneyed and banal and they were happy in their own little fantasy world. He would rather be non indulgent and busily engrossed reading the newspaper, fully loaded with news and information at his disposal. He would daily spend a paisa (cent) to read while everyone else enjoyed the break.

In fact reading was something he loved so much that he would read anything that caught his fancy. He made the optimal use of the limited education he received. None of his companions could understand his passion for reading so they preferred to leave him on his own.

Siraj often with an intention of pulling his leg would tease him by saying "What do you get from reading, doesn't it make you sick? Reading is like coal pasted on paper just looking at it gets me nauseated."

Swaraj would just smile back aware of Siraj's tomfoolery; he would retort "Reading is like exercising the mind, same as we do with our body, the physical work keeps your body fit and fine, reading is like food to the brain, it keeps it thinking and ticking, it increases our vocabulary and expands our knowledge about world and its affairs. And it is better to keep a tab of world affairs then those stupid heroines and their affairs."

To which Siraj quipped "The physical exercise we do all day is more than enough. Why do I fill my mind with crap when all I want is to be in some heroines arm trap?" Swaraj guffawed at Siraj's quick wit and they both had a hearty laugh.

"Ok, I know you won't budge your stand so happy reading." Siraj jocularly added folding his palms in a Namaste. He would leave him to his paper and go to join his group of lesser mortals. Swaraj unperturbed by everybody's indifference would keep reading.

Swaraj knew that Siraj was a prankster, a jester but he was a loyal friend. Besides they enjoyed each other's company and he was blessed to have Siraj by his side.

The group of friends soon realized that leave alone Swaraj, Sandeep would also not mingle with them but for completely different reasons. He would keep himself away from others and would saunter alone, deep in his thoughts.

Sandeep's observation of the city was different from all his coworkers, he soon figured out that no one discriminated one another on the basis of his caste, creed, religion, education, color, character or language and it all got assimilated into just one dimension: class. And the class was determined by the amount of money you carried in your trouser pocket. If you have money you could buy anything you fancied. And it was in our hands to fit in the class that we deemed fit. Do we want to crawl at the bottom, get squeezed in the middle or rise to the top and enjoy the life to the fullest? In the end it all boils down to the power of money. Money determines your position in city; your position in life.

Enough with his sulking at the bottom of the pile, he decided to alter his future. 'Alter' the manager had warned and 'Alter' rang in his ears like a pronouncement.

His careful walk, his contorted facial expressions and sly smiles made it appear that there was something sinister cooking in his mind. His mind began to make all sorts of permutations and combinations. He behaved snobbish and like a restless caged lion desperately waiting for an opportunity to break free. His gait suggested surreptitious intent.

***

In Bombay when it rains, it pours in torrents. The port closes down all its activities for about three months during the season of monsoon as working at port and sea voyage due to inclement weather becomes perilous. And the only sounds that can be heard are the crashing of waves against the boulders and walls and decks of the port, the pandering of rain and the haunting whistle of the sea. There is not a soul to witness the sound and fury of nature. That's the period when the port wears a deserted look.

Most of the workers would go back to their native village during the monsoon. This period coincided with the time when the fields are ploughed and prepared for cultivation. For those who owned farms there would be plenty of work, whereas the others enjoyed their well earned break.

Going back to the village in mid June was an annual ritual, one that everyone looked forward to; families expecting them as well them expecting their families. Before they would leave the men would spend their frugal savings on buying gifts from the city by taking back with them the little joys of city as presents like trunks, bed spreads, inexpensive toys, cheap electronic items almost redundant to city folks but the sellers would make them usable by innovative fix; the same would be with clothes, the second hand, used and discarded clothing was packaged and sold as new and they would take the local delicacies in the form of sweets.

***

Swaraj, Siraj and Sandeep too set off on their journey to their village. It had been three years that Sandeep had joined Swaraj and Siraj. During this time, Sandeep's dislike of Siraj's friendship with Swaraj had intensified and though he would not openly display his displeasure, his body language said it all. Siraj realized this but he disliked Sandeep as well; he was jealous that he was Swaraj's brother and if he would have been given a chance he would undoubtedly had swapped position with him.

The village in all these years too showed some signs of development. The gravel tracks had been tarred. The distance between city and village that looked formidable and stretched was being shrunk and made speedily reachable by bus service and better roads. The school building was finally being constructed. The boundaries that had once divided castes were getting blurred and small establishments selling general provisions had sprouted up.

On the home front, Nirmala had been transformed from a frock-wearing girl to salwar kameez clad young lass. She was fair and slim, beautiful and modest. She kept her hair long and well oiled and parted in the middle and twisted into two braids that were tied with colorful satin ribbons. And the dupatta perched over her head to cover her. Nirmala, in fact, had become the lady of the house.

It had been seven years since Swaraj had left for Bombay and during that period Nirmala passed her matriculation, a big feat for a girl during those times. Kisna was zealous about educating his children. He held views ahead of the times.

She had all her brother's good qualities. She was the lady replica of Swaraj. She was kind and caring, did all the house work, cooked the meals and helped her father in the fields. She was as punctual as the cuckoos bringing food for their chicks and would arrive at the same time everyday carrying a cloth bag with their lunch. The birds would eat on the treetops while they ate it under it branches.

The monsoon break of that year was different. While they were away, Kisna had, with the help of his relatives, found the matches for his three children and had arranged the marriage dates, without their consent or approval. In those days parents had the final say in their children's choice of partner and there would be no question of defiance. Moreover Kisna had confidence in his children.

The custom of dowry and all its accompanying evil was prevalent in those times, Swaraj in his probity was against receiving any dowry or providing dowry for Nirmala's wedding. Kisna supported his decision whole heartedly. But Sandeep revolted, he reasoned "We are two brothers we are both entitled to take dowries. The only dowry that needs to be given is for Nirmala. This is a win-win situation. We will get double while we will have to return only for one; the extra money can be adjusted to settle our marriage expenses."

When Siraj heard about Swaraj's decision for first time he commiserated for Sandeep. He felt Sandeep for the first time suggested something practical according to the circumstances. But it was not to be, Swaraj and Kisna had their strong principles. Their decision was final and abiding. Sandeep demurred but accepted as his mind was occupied by other ideas.

But to make matters worse both brothers had meager savings barely enough to take care of their daily expenses.

Kisna's smooth sail again hit a storm. Marriages require money, and the problem of finance took priority once again. Kisna six acres of land were his only assets, his prized possession that could solve his financial woes.

With time Babulal and Land had become synonymous. His clout had increased in the village and surrounding areas. He was now an MLA of the constituency. He had quit his job and had entered politics. In all these years he had dug his hands deep into politics and had gathered rich pickings. He had avarice for land.

Kisna didn't have to look out for a customer, as Babulal was his prompt buyer. Kisna sold two acres at a throwaway price to fund marriages. The marriages were lavish and gala affairs, unlike the subdued village weddings. Babulal was sent an invitation that he accepted and came to attend the weddings and to bless the couples. Babulal's main intention was to stir the pride of upper caste. His prominent presence in a Brahmin marriage was frowned and furrowed many an eyebrow, even if the other guests disapproved they curtailed their temper into whimper.

Had the law not abolished discrimination, Babulal and his likes would have been thrown out, or as a mark of protest the villagers would have boycotted the dinner party. But his presence indicated acceptability because of the changing times. Babulal was a Netaji so no one dared to oppose his presence, instead he was given preferential treatment which was like adding insult to an injury for the upper caste.

With the culmination of marriages Kisna was joyful and relieved that Swaraj and Sandeep were married and that his liabilities were over.

Devi was Swaraj's partner and Sandeep brought home Rukmini as his wife.

Devi complemented Swaraj with her kind and generous nature, her maturity and intelligence in one so young.

Rukmini was obedient, cultured, an extrovert before marriage but now restrained, quick to adapt and amenable.

But if Devi complemented Swaraj, Rukmini and Sandeep were poles apart.

Both brothers slowly and gradually settled into their married lives.

Two months passed and then it was time again for Swaraj and Sandeep to return to Bombay while Kisna took care of his shrinking farmland.

6

❀

In 1971, it was about nine months after his marriage that Sandeep became father. The news had been posted to him at the manager's address. As in some days it was to be monsoon break and by the time the letter reached the manager making its way through various post offices, Sandeep was back in his village and at that time he came to know about the birth of his son. He named his son Rohan.

In the village Devi and Rukmini efficiently shared the household chores. They would wake up before dawn and would clean and cook, grind the flour, crush the spices, milk the cow, prepare the ghee, wash the cows, clean the barn, gather cow dung to plaster the walls and floor and dry them to make pats to use as cooking fuel. The courtyard now had a well, dug with Swaraj's remittances so now they need not go to village well to wash clothes and utensils. With the well water they would wash the courtyard and verandah and sprinkle the water over the small garden plants. The sisters-in-law in their free time would pick lice, brush and comb, oil and plait hairs while gossiping about whatever would be happening in the village. By the arrival of afternoon they would prepare lunch and carry it to the farm for Kisna where they would together have their lunch. The afternoon hours were a time for a quick nap and after dinner they would retire to their beds well before midnight.

This was their routine; they were contented in their dwellings. Their village was their world. They of course knew about Bombay, and had heard a bit about faraway places such as London, Japan, Pakistan and Lanka but these places existed in their minds as mere names, they had learned about many other countries in their schools but those names had long been forgotten only these were the names that they remembered because London was the place of their previous masters; the British, Pakistan was their hated neighbor and always in news and always for the wrong reasons, Japan because any beautiful girl in their village with slanting eyes and smooth skin was called a Japanese doll and Lanka was made famous by Ramlila. Except for that they knew no more about them, neither did they ever desired of visiting any.

With the brothers back home and add an infant to the family, it was a happy three months reunion.

Bombay was where they returned after three months. Next year it was going to be Swaraj's turn to be blessed with child, this was the news he carried with him to Bombay.

***

Back in Bombay, Sandeep decided to execute his secret plan but was waiting for an opportune moment.

One day the manager assembled all the porters. He announced it with much fanfare, "In a day or two a ship of great proportions is going to dock on our port. It is the mother of all ships. You cannot even imagine its size."

He continued with great excitement. "It's the size even I cannot imagine it is a man made marvel, it's the size of a floating city, the sheer size and passenger capacity would be enormous."

"The ship's capacity would be around 2000 people, it could accommodate 1700 passengers and rest 300 crew members." said the manager rubbing his hands in nervous excitement.

"Because of its enormity it will need deep water to be able to dock and so a collapsible temporary jetty is being prepared at some distance to foray passengers and luggage. The port will be buzzing with activity you will have lots of work. The ship will remain here for three days and will depart on the third evening. We have to show efficiency in how we handle the luggage to make our unit proud." His voice crackled with delight as he was in-charge of such a huge assignment for first time.

He was beaming with pride like a general commanding his troops on the battle field. He wished them good luck and left.

This left the porters dreaming about it size, structure and look; each of them began straddling the horses of their imagination. Sandeep waiting for such an opportunity started weaving plots.

Four days later, the ship arrived at the dock, shining silver and floating like an iceberg on a hot tropical sea, sailing smoothly through the parting sea, its foghorn blaring loud, seeking attention and adulation as its size grew from a dot and reached magnanimity. The ship reached the dock and anchored. Its name appropriately enough was 'Gigantic', rhyming with 'Titanic'.

The ship had two decks and a lower deck almost submerged into the water. The lower deck housed the rest rooms for the crew and cabin staff, ration supplies, housekeeping services, laundry, storage for cargo, room for maintenance spare parts and other such facilities. The first floor had long alleys and rooms on both sides. The top deck had sprawling rooms with portholes on one side. In between there was a swimming pool with a poolside. On the other side was the entertainment zone, children play area, restaurants, bars, boutiques, souvenir shops, and an extensive banquet hall for arranging large parties and shows featuring jugglers, acrobats, magicians, comedians, theatre, music and dance. A special show was planned for every evening.

It was a luxurious ocean liner. The 300 crew included captain, administrator, stewards, stewardess, cabin crew, life guards, sweepers, cleaners and maintenance staff. The female stewards wore simple saris while the men wore white trousers, white long-sleeved shirt that had three dark blue stripes embroidered on the sleeves, a belt at the waist and a maharaja turban with one flap left loose and dangling behind till the buttocks. The stewards comprised the largest members of the crew.

By now Sandeep was thoroughly acquainted with the workings of the dock. On the first two days, there were no passengers on board; the passenger traffic was to come on the third day. The porters were allowed to carry the merchandise up till the entry of the ship on the first deck from there the steward hoisted and transported the goods to their respective spaces.

Sandeep studied the arrangement; he mentally prepared the picture at the port with multitudes of people arriving, their arrival causing clamor, disorder and mismanagement. Then he clicked the sketch of the ship in his mind, counted the number of security guards at the entry point. He calculated the distance and time he would take to reach the entry point past the jetty, if he walked or if he sprinted. He rehearsed his plan.

On the last day the passengers arrived and as usual the porters started loading luggage into ship. In the afternoon, after the lunch break, Sandeep excused himself and went in search of Yeda Bhai who was wandering among the tetrapods exactly at the place where he had expected him to be. Using his hand movement Sandeep indicated to Yeda that he was going to dress him like a bridegroom; he took him to the back and dressed him into a porter's uniform. He picked up his old clothes, pulled out his rings, gathered his clothes and rings and bundled them into a cloth bag that he hid beneath the boulders. He then attached one end of the rope to a heavy stone that he had placed beforehand and the other end to Yeda Bhai's waist.

Yeda Bhai cooperated enthusiastically, unable to judge his intention. Sandeep's next move before he ran off was to push the stone into the water. The stone tumbled down taking with it cluttered litter, pellets and debris along the shore, the huge stone's weight dragged Yeda Bhai into the sea. He juggled, jumbled tried to undo the rope but the moss accumulated on the boulders negated his any last effort to save himself as he skidded and fell into the sea.

In panic, Yeda cried out loud. His shrieks and the sound of the falling debris attracted the ship's occupants - porters, stewards and passengers, for everyone he became the centre of attraction. A commotion was set in, from a distance no one was able to make out what was happening but everyone was captivated and distracted with the going on. The security too left their posts and ran off to join the rest of the audience.

An eerie silence enveloped the port for a while.

As Yeda Bhai immersed into the sea with a loud thud, Sandeep by taking the advantage of the fraction of disturbance and confusion; hopped, skipped and sprinted like a hare by overcoming the oscillating and heaving jetty. He reached the ship's entry point and slipped into the ship unnoticed.

His first part of the plan had worked to perfection. Now he had to blend into the crowd.

***

The ship blew its final siren of departure. The passengers settled; the relatives that had come to see-off shouted their wishes, blew their kisses, had a last stare and bid their frantic good-byes. The ship became a dot in the sea and in sometime it became invisible at it went past the dock.

At the dock, the porters wiping off the sweat from their brows assembled at their sitting place, enjoying their well-deserved break after a hard toil.

Every day they would sit in striking poses: they sprawled or squatted on the ground, stretched their legs to relieve themselves of spasms, they would crack their knees and knuckles the cracking sound proof of their hard work, and some would sit cross legged, others reclined comfortably on their back behind the walls by yawning, taking a siesta, day dreaming or chatting in an animated manner, whereas some cracked jokes.

The butt of their humor that day was the name of the ship. Not a single one of them understood what 'Gigantic' meant. For them it was a tongue twisting name and they took it as a competition to pronounce it correctly. All were faltering and ridiculing each other, some even stuttered out 'Titanic', unknowingly comparing it to the real Titanic.

The other hot topic of discussion that day was the drowning, the arrival of the police, the search for the victim and the futility of the search.

Swaraj as usual was not involved in the discussion. He was somehow neither feeling comfortable reading the news paper. Suddenly or intuitively he enquired in a raised voice in a manner of concern and asked, "Had anybody seen Sandeep?"

Someone remarked, "You very well know that he rarely sits with us. You are at least with us even if you are in your own world, but Sandeep, God know what he thinks of himself. He must be loitering alone somewhere." Swaraj acknowledged the fact with a wry smile.

Swaraj observantly told Siraj, "The saddest sight working at the port is to see emotionally charged farewell by the loved ones of their dear ones with moist eyes, it's very heart-breaking."

Siraj cuts him short, "Now why are you being sentimental? Have you said goodbye to someone today? Otherwise why are you sounding so weird?

Sandeep is not a child, in-fact the air of Bombay has made him more grown up than both of us. He knows the city well than us, don't worry about him and stop being his father" reminded Siraj.

The evening passed quickly, the workers gathered at the mess, and when there was still no sign of Sandeep at dinner that it dawned upon the workers that Sandeep was indeed lost or probably he could be the mystery person that has drowned in the morning's incident.

A frantic search for him began at all the possible places where he could have been found. Fearing that maybe he had drowned, they rushed to the police station.

Siraj however was suspicious, he knew that Sandeep was a good swimmer and could not have drowned easily. The place where the incident took place was far from their working area. And Sandeep had no business being there. He smelt something fishy but went along.

The police were already investigating the mysterious drowning, and now they had the double task of finding Sandeep. The two instances that had happened on the same day, at same place baffled the police.

***

Meanwhile once into the ship, Sandeep's first task was to not get caught because he was still wearing his easily identifiable porter uniform. Sandeep reached the inside tip-toeing and by siding behind every available shield. He was confounded into the maze of architectural marvel. He made his way cautiously and hurriedly. They were empty long alleys with identical doors on either side. He delicately nudged every door with his shoulder to see if any of the one was open. He found one and peeked inside. It appeared to be vacant. He sneaked inside and crouched behind a huge trunk case placed on one end of the room.

It was a pint sized but orderly room, elegantly, richly and beautifully furnished with a narrow single bed and a small attached washroom. A full length mirror was fitted on outside door of the washroom. White curtains, white furnishing and dim lighting created a peaceful ambience. Sandeep plunged himself into the hands of destiny. Even though he was not a firm believer in fate, he fervently prayed to all the deities to keep him safe. He ducked behind the trunk periodically watching from behind the luggage at both the doors waiting his outcome and in-come of the room's occupants. After a while he heard a rattle from inside the washroom and realized that the room that he thought was empty was rather occupied.

A beautiful young girl coming out in a white transparent silk night gown, the fabric silhouetted her rounded hills, she disrobing and slipping into bed bared and naked, so he thought for a moment, his mind took a flight of fancy. He had watched many X-rated Hollywood flicks in shady cinema halls to get excited at the possibility at hand. Then the siren sounded, signaling the departure of Gigantic from Indian shores. The door opened with a creaking sound that he was jolted back from his reverie into reality.

The master of the room, the master of his fate was in front of him. Instead of a beautiful blonde, he saw a middle-aged man. The passenger's name was Mr. Graham Williams. He had been a British officer in India before Independence. Mr. Graham was in his late fifties. He was tall with a fine physique and was neatly dressed. His shirt was tucked into his trousers that were held up by suspenders.

He came out of the washroom, stood in front of the mirror and was starting to remove his clothes as he untied his neck tie, opened his suspenders, undone his shirt buttons, he saw a movement reflected in the mirror. He went and pulled the luggage aside. He nabbed Sandeep hiding behind it.

Sandeep was terrified and broke out in sweat; he was drenched in sweat like a wet cat. He knew that he would be caught sooner or later, but didn't expect it to be so soon, when they were so close to the port. He feared that the ship would turn back and he would be evicted. All his efforts would be in vain.

Mr. Williams towered over him, his two hands in his trousers pockets. He menacingly gazed at Sandeep and barked, "Who are you?" "What are you doing in my room?"

Despite his fear, Sandeep was startled by the fact that the man spoke to him in best of heard Hindi. But Williams knew India very well, having been posted in the country for the better part of his life. He loved India and would often visit it. He was well versed in Hindi and had no problem in communicating with Sandeep.

Sandeep now that he was held and left with no option; looked at him beseechingly, "Sir I am a poor porter in search of better life." His face wore a flaccid look, he whined waiting to see Mr. William's reaction.

Williams took a few steps, pacing the room trying to figure out Sandeep's motives. Sandeep watching him, cunningly suggested, "Sir, take me with you as your servant I will always be indebted to you."

Williams stared at him with sharp eyes like piercing a dragger into Sandeep's any hope of making it through. Yet for once Mr. Williams was lured into the plea; after all he had always been pampered by servants when he lived in India during the Raj.

Finally he said, "Ok, sleep here tonight and I will decide what to do about you in the morning".

Sandeep was relieved that he was not kicked out of the room, or been handed to the administration; he was happy that by the time morning comes they would be well and truly away from Bombay port and deep into the sea and so for him alone the ship will not go back to the port. He would finally be taken to England and then he will wait and watch his fate.

Next morning ruminating long and hard Williams said, "Alright, I will handle the situation. But first I'll have to come up with a convincing tale; otherwise you'll be caught and deported back to your country. Don't utter a word until I say. Just stay put in your position."

Williams went to the housekeeping section and bribed a steward to give him a pair of uniforms and some other clothes.

Williams gave the uniforms to Sandeep, and said, "Pretend to be my personal steward and follow me everywhere."

After some days passed lying low, Sandeep went along with Mr. Williams wearing steward clothes. He averted curious and questioning glances of other stewards as they could not recognize him to be part of their tribe.

One day when the ship had completed half its journey. Williams devised a plot with a creativity of a playwright. He explained Sandeep of how to play along, "When you see me accidently drop some papers overboard run up to me and make a desperate attempt to catch hold of the papers, the act should look genuine, but be careful." He stopped, smiled and said, "Or should I say, be careless, and do not catch any, let them fly into the sea. This will make look the scene look real and would be held as testimony of our attempts of trying to retrieve the papers."

Mr. Williams would turn the table fan in his room to full speed, make the papers fly and make Sandeep practice before he put his plan into action.

One fine breezy day, Williams took Sandeep on the upper deck. He sat beside the poolside arranging scrap papers in a file. As he was shuffling them around, he acted as if a gust of wind had blown the papers away by himself flinging papers into the sea.

Williams ran towards the administrator explaining that his servant's important immigration documents had accidently fallen into the sea and were now lost. While Sandeep made a hue and cry that what will happen of him as the documents were scattered far into the sea and were irretrievable.

The officer asked, "What were you doing with such important documents by the poolside?"

Williams replied, "I am short sighted and the room is dimly lit. I wanted to get his papers in order before we reached Britain to avoid any last minute scampering, particularly since he doesn't speak English. But the winds blew them away like freed birds." He joked.

The administrator made a note of this episode and conformed Sandeep's presence on the ship, thereby making it legal and making Williams certain that his spurious claim has worked to perfection.

This assurance was enough for Sandeep now that his destination was within his reach. Mr. Williams told Sandeep to call him always as 'Sir'. Casual interaction continued every day. Three months journey was long enough to get him know all about Sandeep.

Thus Sandeep sailed into an unknown new world, a new life and a new beginning.

7

❋

Back at the port, the rescue team and the police team continued to search for that elusive body. Six days had passed without results. However on the seventh day they found a body a whole week after the drowning.

The body lay squeezed between the sea bed and under the weight of two huge stones. One stone that was tied to his waist had upturned on the body; while luckily for Sandeep the other stone had somehow tumbled fell and rested on Yeda and covered his full body, and that was the reason his body was not recovered for so many days even after intense combing.

It was the sight of fingers emerging from under the rocks that had alerted the rescuers.

The recovered body was in a highly decomposed state, wrapped in scum and algae, putrescent, emanating wafts of acrid smell, fish and sea creatures had nibbled parts of flesh, the eyes had popped out. The matted hair had been washed and smoothened but the face had been disfigured beyond recognition. The identification process had become extremely difficult.

It was only the tattered porter's uniform with badge number and the rope that bore a barely visible mark of his porter number, helped them ascertain that the dead man was Sandeep. The height and body structure too resembled his.

The cops took everyone to the police station and interrogated them one by one.

Siraj at first objected, "Sir, he can't drown."

Inspector, "How can you be so sure about it?"

"Because he had no business to be at the place where the drowning took place"

"Do you have any proof?"

"No sir but he was wily and clever"

"That doesn't spare him from drowning" said the inspector as he eyed him with curiosity.

"He could have vanished somewhere or maybe lost but he can't drown because he was a good swimmer in our village river"

"To swim in river and to swim in the sea is a different world altogether."

The police dismissed Siraj's arguments and ended their enquiry after the manager's, eye witnesses and porter's version. They saw no reason in anybody's objection, yet to make their work simple and to expediently solve the matter, they with their shoddy and lethargic investigation concluded that the murder could be over some family dispute. Swaraj was only his near and dear one and the only one who could have any motive so based on these flimsy grounds, they arrested Swaraj by taking him into preventive custody.

Siraj protested, "Isn't to convict Swaraj without proof scandalous."

"Oh, so now you are going to teach us law, if we want you in the cell, even though you are pure as angel we can frame charges of pissing in a public place and take you into custody. And then that truly would be scandalous" He said menacingly.

"So before laying blame on us, you go and get the proof."

"And you are sympathizing with Swaraj. You are very much involved in the case, I have gathered from sources that both of you are thick as thieves. Thank good lord that I am leaving you or you too could be booked as an aide."

Siraj was aghast as to how the facts were manipulated, but still not convinced of Sandeep's death. He put in his best arguments to convince them of their botched investigation but it was of no help. The police instead scared Siraj of worst consequences, he was petrified.

When Swaraj saw him getting entangled into the web of law without his fault and silenced with threat of arrest for rightfully arguing, he urged him to gather evidence of his innocence. He told him, "I am in custody, but you are free and my only hope to find out the truth."

Kisna was too old to understand the complexities of law or to handle life in a big city. He agreed to arrange for the finances and told Siraj to look into every aspect of law to get Swaraj's early release.

Siraj leaned against the wall dejected and exhausted, reliving in his thoughts the days of how much they enjoyed the leisure hours and the entertainment provided by Yeda Bhai. At that very moment he was struck by a thought. He started recollecting the event of the day of drowning. He remembered seeing Yeda bhai at the port premises but since then there had been no trace even of him anywhere. His heart pounded heavily at the hope, he had found light at the end of tunnel. He decided to follow his instincts. He discussed his idea with the manager.

The manager agreed and sanctioned him some free time each day to carry on with his pursuit. Thus Siraj started his parallel investigation. He began his enquires in the slums by gathering information about the whereabouts of Yeda Bhai.

Could he be ill?

Had he left the slums to wander elsewhere?

Had anyone seen him in the past few days?

To all his queries the answer till now was in the negative.

From the day of drowning no one had seen Yeda Bhai. This brightened his resolve and hope. He had a gut feeling that the dead person was no other than Yeda.

His second clue was that Yeda Bhai wore many finger rings and the body that had been fished out of the sea had none. Might be the rings could have slipped out of his fingers onto the sea bed, so if he could find them, then his mission would have a direction.

He shared his doubts with the manager and asked if some porters could volunteer in the search operation to find the rings near the spot where the body was found. He hired the rescue divers by agreeing to pay their fees.

The divers swilled the sea bed while the porter friends combed the boulders and after their intensive search, they found the cloth bag.

Meanwhile, the police were doing their work; they had taken Sandeep's medical report from the manager's office and checked his blood type with the body's the blood group did not match.

Siraj was now equipped with proof that Yeda Bhai had disappeared from the slums and his clothes and rings had been found near the port.

The police had also discovered that the blood groups were different.

Besides Siraj deposited the certificates earned by Sandeep in local village competitions that evidenced that Sandeep was a skilled swimmer.

Moreover, there were enough witnesses who could vouch for Swaraj's clean character.

So after running from pillar to post, Siraj's endurance had paid off and Swaraj was released.

The body that was found was that of Yeda Bhai.

His clothes and rings were found.

The motive could have been settling of old rivalries.

Amidst all the unsolved riddles, there were many moot questions.

What was Sandeep's connection with Yeda?

Where was Sandeep?

How did Yeda adorn Sandeep's uniform?

Why were Yeda's clothes and rings tied in a cloth bag and hidden within the boulders?

There were questions galore, but answers to none.

Swaraj was released but with the warning that he would remain under scrutiny till Sandeep's disappearance was shrouded in mystery.

By now corruption had become rampant; the unleashing of British Raj was like a free opening for people in power like the vultures attacking the carcass after the lion's share. Kisna had firsthand experience of how it worked among the bureaucracy, now he did see how the police department used it. The bug of corruption by now had bitten every aspect of Indian life.

Despite the character certificate from the village panchayat, the posting of bail, the fact that there was no concrete proof against Swaraj; palms were still needed to be greased.

The lawyer, whom Siraj had approached to get bail, explained, "Once you are in a police net, you have three options, either pay and get released; either have influence and get released or have proper connections and get released. There is no way else."

He explained, "You know the day the police system was created, Devil celebrated and partied; and declared to the world 'Congratulate me, for today I too have become a father.'"

Siraj quizzed, "So you mean to say that police are the children of devil."

"Yes dear and we too are included for we have the ability to screw the innocent and bail-out criminals. But we are not brutal and a little decent then them. You can call us devil's step children." The lawyer laughed at his own expense.

"If you want your friend freed, arrange for the bail amount, my fees and police's bribe.'

The freedom for Swaraj had cost Kisna dearly. The expenses incurred for the personal investigation, arranging for bail amount, lawyer fees, bribe to the police, loss of income since Sandeep had disappeared and Swaraj was in jail meant that the only alternative was to sell more land while Babulal unconditionally held the only prerogative.

Kisna went to Babulal's home. Kisna was the same old Kisna, what changed, in fact was Babulal. His opulence amazed Kisna. He admired his without guilt appetite to digest country's wealth, his subjugating power over the people; the power of his chair, the supplication of sycophants and servants servitude.

He had seen an era of zamindar and remembered Banne Nawab's days of notoriety and prominence of power. Babulal was a modern day zamindar. The title had changed the job was the same: to suck people's blood.

Babulal now owned large tracts of land, prime properties in posh localities in big cities, owned mines, controlled educational institutions, his firms handled government contracts. He had become the master, from being landless he became a landlord, from underprivileged he was now the undisputed king of the area, from a pawn in the hands of the upper caste he became a kingmaker in a new India, from lowly he became exalted, from flat bellied he turned pot bellied. His garb changed as well. He discarded his western outfit for silk kurtas, crisp dhotis and Nehru caps.

His change was dynamic and was now the face of the ruling class. He contested elections from reserved seat, thereby minimizing the competition. Babulal held the nerves of the masses; he gave the war-cry that 'Do not cast your vote, but vote for your caste'. He took the voters into confidence by scaring them that the government would take away their reservation, if he was not selected to defend them their rights. He would promise them that come what may he will not let the right to reservation end till his last breath.

The voters didn't mind how corrupt he was until he was the one who represented his caste. The baton of power had moved from upper class to lower class, sowing the seeds of caste based politics.

Kisna had sold another acre of land. Sandeep's loss and then the turn of events made him so depressed that he suffered a paralytic attack and was bedridden.

Kisna's life was juxtaposed of happiness following sorrow, always in tandem.

When Swaraj was born, his land had been confiscated and in the process of regaining it he had sacrificed two acres; when Sandeep was born there was drought and he was forced to go to city; when Nirmala was born, his wife died; when Rohan was born Sandeep disappeared and when Swaraj's son was born Swaraj was languishing in jail, Swaraj was demoralized by police indifference, atrocious behavior and his wrong confinement; this broke Swaraj and Kisna became paralytic.

Every birth had brought with it a new birth of problems.

Swaraj was stunned by this cruel twist of fate, he looked skywards and muttered, "Sandeep has gone, father is paralyzed, besides my family I have Sandeep's to take care of and now there are father's medical expenses. I am the sole breadwinner now, how am I to go through this phase of my life?" He took a deep breath and sighed despondently, "Maybe God is testing me by giving me these problems; maybe he will also provide solutions."

Realizing that nothing would be gained feeling sorry for himself, he shook off his upset mood and remembered Siraj's wise advice, he started with his work again.

He remembered that two months after they had resumed their work at the port returning from the monsoon break, Gigantic had docked and rocked his world. That cursed day Sandeep had disappeared, he had been put behind bars and had lost his wages, and he was thankful that he had survived because of the manager's kindness and measly contributions from his fellow porters. But now survival was becoming burdensome and exiguous.

In order to earn some additional money, to bring some semblance of order back into life, Swaraj decided to work some extra hours. The duty at the port would begin at 10 a.m. Thus, he would begin his day early by delivering newspapers, washing the vehicles of the officers residing in the nearby naval area, he took on the work to clean, swab and dust the shops before they opened for business.

Delivering newspapers had a perk, since Swaraj was an avid reader and would read the papers without spending the one anna he used to, with an added perk of variety of news items from various newspapers to choose from.

Siraj was Swaraj's companion and would join him in the morning tasks. In this way he too earned some extra bucks.

One day while they were cleaning one of the shops, Swaraj saw something and slightly shook his head with a wry smile. Siraj who was quick to notice, he whispered, "Hey mate, what's the matter? Why are you smiling in such a manner?"

Swaraj replied, "As you know, I am a Brahmin and, in good old days or not so long ago, only Dalits did the menial work. Now I am doing the same for a Dalit."

Siraj paused with his work with broom in hand and mopping rag on his shoulder wondering of what Swaraj thought and waited expectedly for him to explain what he meant. But when he didn't and got back to work, confused and anxious to know, Siraj asked impatiently and perplexedly, "How do you know that the shopkeeper is a Dalit?" in a hushed tone to avert the attention of the shop owner.

Swaraj nudged Siraj and looked pointedly towards the garlanded portrait of Dr. Babasaheb Ambedkar hanging on the wall above the counter and the incense sticks placed on either side of it. "For the down trodden he is like a godly figure as well as the father of our constitution."

He continued, "Today I have really understood the meaning of Independence. Our constitution and growing urbanization has emancipated the underprivileged" He playfully flicked Siraj on the back of his head and remarked, "I always told you to read, it keeps you updated and knowledgeable."

Siraj laughed, "You have opened my eyes brother. I should really start reading because whenever I looked at the photograph I thought it to be the owner's father's portrait. Instead he has turned out to be the father of our constitution." He cackled while Swaraj giggled faintly so as not to offend the shop owner.

Siraj continued "Yes bro, the underprivileged are gaining ground rapidly. Look at our Netaji Babulal and how he has succeeded through his ill gotten gains."

Swaraj corrected Siraj's myopic assessment of what he actually meant to say, "The success you are mocking is few and far between. The vast majority of underprivileged in rural areas are still been harassed and deprived of their rights. In cities however, they are part of a large mass of people that blankets the segregation of caste, religion, ethnicity into anonymity. The solace for them today is that at least in urban areas they are constitutionally protected and uplifted."

Unable to digest Swaraj's verbosity, Siraj jokingly held his head from spinning out of control and pretended to faint.

To avoid shopkeeper's rebuke because of their giggles and blabbers they quickly finished their work and left the shop still giggling and when they were well past the shop they had a hearty laugh.

Months passed in a pattern and then the monsoon arrived. Swaraj went back to his village and saw his infant son. He named him Arun (meaning sun) and wished that his life would be as bright as the sun.

8

✳

As the ship neared the port, taking a vista from the deck of the ship, Sandeep had his first view of Britain. He noticed the crystal clear turquoise waters of the ocean, the well-behaved passengers and crowd at the port, the organized management of the port, all so very different from the chaos and confusion of India. There was no pushing or jostling, the passengers patiently formed a queue and by following the signboards, moved slowly towards the immigration counters.

He followed Mr. Williams, and when it was his turn, the polite officer at the other end asked him with a smile, "Hello gentleman, can I have a look at your passport please?" Sandeep kept his gaze lowered and ignored the question as if he had heard nothing. The custom officer repeated.

Sandeep gave a cursory look towards Mr. Williams as he had been instructed not to utter a word without his consent.

At that very moment Mr. Williams intervened, "Excuse me officer, he is my servant and I have lost his documents at sea. The administrator has evidence of this mishap." His elitist mien, his calm and authoritative voice, left the officer with no courage or suspicion to probe further, but to dispatch the case to his immediate superior.

Those were the days when illegal migration and large scale migration was not the case so the immigration laws were not so strict and after a round of discussions they called upon the administrator to give his side of the story.

He said, "Mr. Williams reported to me of having lost his servants documents, we went through our passenger's list and found that there was no record of a ticket being sold to someone by the name of Sandeep. Moreover, the count of passengers had increased by one. But why would Mr. Williams intend to save Mr. Sandeep? What would Mr. Williams gain by standing in Mr. Sandeep's favour? Why would he save his skin by standing in the line of fire? Moreover, it could be that due to large count of passengers we may have made a mistake."

The official enquired, "What kind of a mistake?"

"We would have issued two tickets to Mr. Williams by the same name and would have counted it as one and then there was an incident at the entry point at the time when the passengers were entering so there could have been a deflection of attention that could have caused a mistake."

"Yes, yes it was at the time when there was chaos that we had made our entry" said Williams excitedly and confidently.

"So with due respect to Mr. Williams, he should be given time to put together his servant's documents once again" concluded the administrator.

The administrator's clean-chit left the ball in Mr. William's court. To save his prestige as well as to avoid going against the law, he was given three months to prove that Sandeep was his servant and that his entry was legal.

Till then the port invigilators detained Sandeep on charges of lack of documents and entering the country illegally. He was transferred to minimum security asylum seekers detention centre.

Refugees were treated like scum. Their entry was seen as a burden on the host country leading to an increase in population, hate-crimes, racial abuse, poverty and other social ills.

At the centre, Sandeep was served sub-standard food, starved, beaten, kicked and humiliated. The attendant took a liking for Sandeep. He was attracted by his wheatish complexion, taut body and youth. He provocatively sang.

"So dear, come near.

You want to settle here.

Why? Is this your father's house.

You dirty little Indian mouse,

The burning fire in me you will douse.

Let's play spouse-spouse."

He was pulled by his hair and subjected to buggery. They took the hell out of him.

Every inmate had to endure some or the other kind of abuse and humiliation in order to escape worse conditions back home or by their desire to settle in developed country.

Sandeep tolerated the torture by pinning his hopes on Mr. Williams promise to get him released, otherwise after all the humiliation he would return to square and if Mr. Williams didn't keep his word he would be deported.

On his part, Williams perhaps to save his honor or avoid arrest for fraud and to turn his fiction into truth used his contact in the Indian embassy to arrange for bogus and forged documents to ensure Sandeep's release. Finally he presented before the authorities fake passport, fake work permit and fake identity and got Sandeep released.

Mr. Williams took Sandeep to his palatial mansion outside London, in the country.

He did not have a gatekeeper, so he opened the huge iron gates with a long creaking sound and drove through a long passage with a huge garden beside.

He first stopped at the servant quarter, which was to become Sandeep's room. It had a single bed with a quilt and pillows. Besides it was a small side table and a night lamp kept on it. There was a wardrobe and attached washroom. Curtains adorned the windows. Everything placed at its place, everything looked clean and neat. But as far as Sandeep was concerned, he did not have to share the room with anyone.

Just a few months ago; In India forget the luxury of a room he didn't have a proper place to sleep. Rats and cats shared his space; there were lizards crawling on the walls, insects nibbled on the legs. The sub-human conditions in detention center were still an unnerving thought, fresh in his mind. But now everything had changed and he felt as if he was in heaven, with a stroke of luck his past life changed beyond his belief. He thanked god for giving him the chance to meet Mr. Williams and for the new direction his life had taken.

His room was just a trailer for the main picture.

When Mr. Williams opened the doors to his villa, what he saw was splendor. He gaped at his plush interiors, the wooden flooring covered here and there with Persian carpets, the exquisite couches in the magnanimous hall and one set of mahogany sofa near the giant fire place, and an aquarium teeming with exotic species of fish on one side of the wall. The villa was a duplex and the hall had a curved stairs on both sides leading up to the first floor; the walls were decorated with priceless paintings with antique artifacts arranged in alcoves. A crystal chandelier was suspended from the roof above a central seating area. On the opposite wall was the first copy of the Monalisa, her enigmatic smile enhanced the beauty of the hall.

Then he was shown the big garage with its collection of vintage cars.

From a hovel Sandeep found himself transported into a palace. He rubbed his eyes, pinched himself to make sense of what he was seeing. He was stunned by the affluence of his surroundings.

Sandeep's life changed dramatically and so did his behavior. He urgently removed the plastic-covers from the couches and began to dust with a piece of cloth; he scrubbed the floor, changed water of the fish tank. He shined the room in no time. He suddenly waked from his slumber and became a live wire from a sloth. He was shrewd enough to realize that it would be to his advantage to impress his master, so leaving no stone unturned he took the decision to work diligently to keep Mr. Williams happy.

Mr. Williams had a part time butler at his service. But after a while he terminated his services. He loved Indian food and surprisingly, Sandeep had a hidden talent of a cook, he turned out to be an excellent cook and produced many tasty curries, korma, kebabs, koftas, pulaos and various types of rotis.

Sandeep was a vegetarian but he never showed his reluctance to cooking non-vegetarian food. In fact, he soon began eating meat, fish and chicken. He had compromised his dharma for his karma.

His main intention, however, was to carry out all the tasks his master gave him; to obey all his commands so that he would be impressed by his efficiency and enterprise. As result besides cooking, washing and cleaning, he took over the gardener's job. He got the gardener dismissed and clutched his job also.

Soon Mr. Williams taught him driving to save on the driver's salary, and the chauffeur's role was added to his long unending list of chores.

After he learnt driving, Mr. Williams patted on his shoulders and said cheeringly, "Now you have become my man-Friday, the man for all seasons; the man for all reasons."

On hearing these words of appreciation, Sandeep blushed like a child and covered his face in embarrassment, back home if the dock manager had uttered the same words, Sandeep would have contemptuously brushed the statement aside.

Mr. Williams shared a love-hate relationship with India. On one hand he would praise India for its mysticism, religiosity, diversity, food, their culture of showing overwhelming gratitude towards guest. But at the same time he slammed her poverty, orthodoxy, superstition, religious bigotry and climate. He had something or the other to say about India and Indians.

Mr. Williams was an elderly, divorcee without children, he had accumulated great wealth that he had invested heavily in stocks and bonds and they were his source of income.

Just after dinner and before they retired for sleep; and after Sandeep would have finished his day's duty. They both would spend time together drinking. Sandeep took liking to the smooth, light and silky English liquor and Mr. Williams took the role of Indian indoctrinator.

One night during their regular drinking session he asked, "Do you know why India got independence?"

Sandeep mouthed a standard schoolboy answer, "Yes sir, because Indians fought for it"

"Bullshit, British left India because it had become a muddle, was in disarray and the World War II had drained Britain of its resources." He continued after a sip "I was part of the governing system, and the exchequer no longer deemed it viable to rule India, nothing was left to be squeezed. India had been scrapped to the skeleton. The people were agitated and fighting on religious lines; the seed of Divide and rule that we had sprinkled had grown into a mammoth jungle and subsequently into a jungle fire out of everybody's control. British were desperate to have the monkeys off their backs. British didn't free India; they let India loose".

And then he would pinch Sandeep's pride, "And look at your servant mentality, you came behind us, shaking dog's tail and that too in droves to serve us all over again."

On another occasion he did start again, "Do you know, what a Kohinoor is?"

Sandeep with his limited knowledge said it with a grin, "I know of only one Kohinoor, the Kohinoor chachi of our village."

Williams laughed out loud and said, "You fool, Kohinoor is the diamond, it was your diamond but it is now in our possession. It is worth enough to wipe off your debts, but here you Indians take pride in wiping off our asses."

Such words of scorn demeaning him and India would hurt Sandeep's self-worth. But Mr. Williams would balance it off with peppered words of praise for Indians by saying, "Sandeep you are a loyal servant, Indians have the virtue of loyalty ingrained in their blood" and similarly; often in jolly mood, he would mentor Sandeep on stocks and investments, carelessly passing insider tips.

Sandeep had grown wiser about India then all his years in school put together and had fair knowledge about share market and investment options. Initially he adapted to the idea of sharing a peg or two with Mr. Williams.

But gradually the walls of the villa appeared to grow taller and taller and moving closer and closer, it began to choke him for space. His contact with outside world was limited till the gates of the villa; to receive postal checks, share related letters and bank statements and occasional drive to downtown with Mr. Williams to purchase groceries, daily supplies and visit to the bank. Otherwise there would be just two souls trapped in a large estate.

After three and half years, Sandeep's loneliness intensified and to break the monotony of life within William villa he yearned to bring his family with him. By then he had known Mr. Williams thoroughly and gained his confidence, the elderly man was wholly dependent on him.

One day at favorable moment he asked Mr. Williams, "Sir, I wish to go to India to bring back my wife and child back with me."

Wondering at his proposition Mr. Williams asked, "Why? How come you are suddenly missing your family after so many years" Spreading his hands wide he said, "You wanted better life? Aren't you getting it? Then why do you want to go back?"

Sandeep artfully replied, "Sir, I wanted to settle myself first and now that I am settled and under your shelter. I want to bring them with me."

Sandeep had mastered the act of smarming and he knew that blandishment is what Mr. Williams would easily fall for.

He then added ingratiatingly, "My wife and I can both work for you, in this way you'll get two servants for the pay of one."

Mr. Williams had a large estate to look after. He secretly admired Sandeep's commitment and how he had single handedly managed his property and resources so frugally. More so being thrift he promptly agreed but cautioned

Sandeep with a condition, "Return as soon as possible or don't come back", he said firmly.

"If you return within six months I'll help to make you and your family UK citizens." He said with a purpose of sticking out a carrot to the rabbit, carrot which Sandeep would not let go of easily.

Sandeep and Mr. Williams shared a relationship where both had become dispensable to one another. Sandeep who wanted to forget his past was living the life he could only dream of; enjoying the facilities even though he had to slog endlessly juggling all the duties of the household.

Mr. Williams on the other hand wanted to retain Sandeep at any cost because where else could he have found such cheap labor in prosperous Britain where staff was so expensive, and for everything there was a separate servant service, Butler, chauffeur, gardener, maid, gate keeper, caretaker. Here Sandeep was all molded into one. So he allured him with his offer.

It would take five months to travel to and fro from London to Bombay by ship, which was much cheaper then air travel. Mr. William's condition was that he must return within six months, the extra period of one month allowed him to spend with his extended family and get the passports ready while he contacted the British consulate in Bombay and made arrangements for them to expedite the visas so that there would be no delay in his return.

9

Sandeep set on his voyage to India. When he reached Bombay port he noticed that not a thing had changed since he had left. There was the same nauseating ordour of stale fish, the noisy, filthy, unhygienic, pungent fish market, the paan stained walls, chaos and poverty all around with slums and shanties of the fisherman's colonies, the dhows and dilapidated launches of private contractors sailing in unclean water, the boats specked like dirty dots floating on sea surface, the humidity, the stench of perspiration and the same old faces.

The first face he saw was his brother's. Swaraj had not changed much.

Swaraj didn't recognize Sandeep because he had changed completely and he always had attitude, and now combined with attire had completely changed his personality; besides he wasn't expecting to see him.

Sandeep hesitatingly and somewhat reluctantly called out to Swaraj, Swaraj looked elsewhere a bit disconcerted, when he saw this well dressed sahib standing right in front of him.

Sandeep again called out his name, unsure that he had heard him right, he gave his ear a stir, disbelieving his ears and eyes; and then recognition dawned. His eyes lit up with joy and he gave him a tight hug, which Sandeep disliked but he had no option but to reciprocate.

The news that Sandeep was alive and had returned spread like wildfire through the port. All his co-workers encircled him, one was scratching his head, the other one his beard, and some were eyeing him with wide eyes like idiots; while some with complete astonishment.

That was the year a movie named 'Sagina' was released and except Swaraj everyone else being movie buffs had watched the movie. Their favourite superstar Dilip Kumar had performed a song wearing an English style suit, a hat and a stick in hand. He was shabbily dressed in the movie. But here in front of them was an improved version of Dilip Kumar, in a spick and span long overcoat and a necktie, a bowler hat, ironed trousers, highly mirror shined shoes and a leather bag in hand. His cheeks were red as an apple; he had a fair Indian skin. He looked a mixture of Indian in an English garb.

"He is not Sandeep. He could be a prankster playing with the emotions of poor Swaraj" said someone.

"Yes maybe because Swaraj had not watched the recent movie and so he could be fooled easily".

"Oh wait. He could be an imposter" exclaimed another.

To which other one remarked, "Move aside, you dumb, who you think Swaraj is? Is he a king that someone would want to be related to him or for that matter, what is this sahib going to extract by being a relative to a humble coolie."

The answer made everyone thinking that obviously what would a sahib gain by being an imposter, so after a pause someone seriously questioned, "Then who is this masquerade?"

After a flurry of doubts and questions and with Sandeep providing correct answers, they were convinced that he was indeed their own Sandeep. They were taken aback by his change in luck and look.

One patted the back of other complimenting him for their joint acumen, he hissed, "We had aptly named him 'Chameleon' he is indeed the one of the finest quality" spreading a bout of laughter among the surprised congregation.

Sandeep was averse at meeting them. His aristocracy belied of his servility towards Mr. Williams. He was revolted by their sweaty shirts, smelly armpits bloated with sweat, pungent onion like body ordour. His proximity to Mr. Williams had given him a false sense of his own status. Forgetting that till recently he had been one of them, but now so much had changed or it was a paradox of change.

Siraj had been perspicaciously observing the going-on from the distance. When the bustle settled down, he came forward to shake Sandeep's hand and exchange pleasantries. He was devoid of any interest of his sudden reappearance because he knew that the true story from his side would never be told.

Siraj always with Swaraj's good faith in mind turned to him and reminded him, "Listen now that Sandeep is back the first thing you must do is to go to the police station and get your name cleared and seek closure to the case that is hanging like a sword on your head."

Swaraj nodded and the three of them went to the police station. In between the way Siraj explained the reason for their urgent visit to the police station.

In police files their case was old and ordinary, with the dead person being yesteryear don turned insane and the lost person a lowly coolie. The file had got piled and pressed; covered with dust and cobwebs. The beat constables of the station knew Swaraj and they had kept the case alive so that they could harass Swaraj and extract money from him every month.

The senior inspector asked for the file. Siraj and Swaraj were instructed to sit on the wooden bench outside his cabin while Sandeep was called inside his office to be interrogated.

He got him comfortably seated. He sized up his client and was least interested in unraveling the mystery of his disappearance and re-appearance. For him here was a new prey from which he could extract money.

But Sandeep had been hardened by his experience of being questioned at every instance. He had faced countless questions in the past, first from Mr. Williams, then the immigration officials and at the asylum. So it no longer mattered when it was the turn of Indian police officer to have a go. He had turned into seasoned interviewee. He was relaxed, calm, composed and prepared for the onslaught.

The officer, screwing and pulling wax from his ears with a blunt lead pencil started, "So Sir, you worked as a porter with your brother, then what kind of conjuring act you performed that you drowned as a mamooli coolie and come back sailing as a Mister?"

Sandeep knew that the case was forgotten and his story was of little interest. In hindsight he had summed up that the inspector's only interest was to make some money. His large and pot belly, his way of questioning and his look indicted at his lust for money. So he went ahead with his brief and concocted account of how he had vanished.

"On the day when Gigantic docked at the port, I along with the others started our daily routine, but when I was inside the ship. I stumbled and hit upon something hard, I cried out loud but no one heard. As I was losing consciousness I hazily remember that there was some disorder and everyone had got interested in that and after a while I lost consciousness. When I regained consciousness the ship had already left the port. An Englishmen took me under his wings. What transpired in the interlude is out of my knowledge. I went with him to his country. He was not willing to let me come back home, but I insisted, so here I am."

To give creditability to his tale he added, "If I would be at fault, why would I have returned back?" He smiled weakly, giving an expression to the officer to think about it.

The officer clapped mockingly, "Good; Very well said Mister. Your story deserves an ovation. What do you think, we are fools? He banged his hands on the desk and said, "If we want we can solve crimes with the snap of our fingers. But we do so or not is another matter altogether."

He guffawed at his own wit. "In your case, there was also a man who drowned on the day you disappeared."

Feigning ignorance Sandeep stuttered a bit in his reply, "So what, what do I have to do with it. It can be a coincidence." He coolly questioned back, "Can't it be?"

Inspector continued, "Oh, I love coincidences and dear sir for your fabricated tale. I would give it ten on ten, almost perfect but for an oversight." The officer circled his chair, knocked his fist into his cupped other hand, leaned forward and after a moment of silence said, "The body that we fished out was not you, you prove it with your presence, but then how did it wear your uniform, have your badge number, your rope. We found Yeda Bhai's clothes carefully packed and concealed behind the rocks. There has to be a strong connection, it can't be a coincidence, your little lie will need a lot of explaining."

Sandeep understood that his deception wouldn't work anymore so he directly came to the point, "What will be the price of your help to cut the matter short and close it forever?"

The Inspector appeared startled "You are blatantly confessing to your crime without worrying about the repercussions, but at the same time you are offering me a price for a cover up."

Sandeep looked confused to find such an upright officer in the rotting system of corruption. But the inspector didn't let his doubts linger long. He added, "Don't be nervous dear, we are not used to such direct offerings, instead it is us who make the first move. This was just a bluff devised to fright you a bit."

Heaving a sigh of relief, Sandeep stated, "You quote your price and I'll tell you my condition."

The inspector quoted his price and Sandeep specified what he needed to be done and told the inspector that he wanted all of it to be done in less than a month's time.

The Inspector agreed that it was a simple open and shut case. After all the case was of no national importance where the result would give him promotion or make him a hero. He was not hard pressed to deliver the result. There was no media scrutiny.

The dead man had no relatives, no family, no one cared for him and no one cried. He had no sanity, no future and no one had registered a complaint and now that Sandeep had been found the file could be closed by mentioning that the missing person had been found and the case of death could be put down as accidental.

Only a little bit of formalities were required so they haggled about the amount for a while and then it was all settled.

The Inspector and Sandeep came out of the cabin beaming. They shook hands and waved good bye. Siraj and Swaraj who were seated on the bench outside the cabin, couldn't comprehend what had conspired between them, but assumed that the case had finally been sorted.

The monsoon was still another month away, so Siraj stayed back while the brothers left for their village.

Swaraj always travelled back to the village in an overcrowded general compartment, filled to the capacity. He would seat steady and squeezed at any available place unable to maneuver his body movements and would remain constrained to the confined space. Let alone, be able to leave for the need to attend to nature's call. But he had got used to this way of traveling, so when Sandeep bought two second class tickets Swaraj was happy at his elevation in status and looked forward to the taste of luxury.

If Sandeep had been alone he would have definitely travelled first class. Even though he was just a servant in London and doing the same level of work as he was doing back in India, he could still afford it because of the difference of a paper note with change of print from Reserve Bank of India to Bank of England; the conversion rates of a pound went a long way when converted into rupees. But he didn't want to show-off fearing that Swaraj may ask for a favor, so he settled for two second class tickets. He purchased Swaraj a set of clothes so that he appeared presentable.

Swaraj was thrilled that Sandeep was back and poured his heart out to him, letting him know each and every event that occurred during his absence. He explained in anecdotes all the big and small stories that had happened in the past five years he was away. He was oblivious in his excitement to understand Sandeep's in-brewing treachery and his exit plan.

Sandeep nodded and muttered, pretending to show an interest. Whenever Swaraj asked him any questions about his life in Britain, Sandeep pretended not to hear, he skipped, ignored or gave laconic or evasive answers, guarding himself against inquisition. He neither elucidated the reason for his sudden disappearance or the cause and course of his reappearance.

Back at the village the entire household happily welcomed him back. He was unconcerned about their love and affection, but eager to pack his bags and move out in haste.

His five years in Britain had made him contemptuous of his humble background and the state of the house appalled him. He wanted to move out and stay in the nearby city. He was aware of his past; however, the main reason for his displeasure at staying in the house was; how to secretly organize passports for Rukmini and Rohan.

With the help of facilitators and agents and liberal use of bits of papers called currency, he got the passport within a few days. At the same time he received the news through long-distance calling service installed at the village post office, that the missing person case had been closed.

It was now time to make his move,

Sandeep without a tinge of hesitancy in his voice announced to his family, "I am going back to Britain with just my wife and son, that too for good and forever."

Swaraj was stunned and disheartened by his decision. He angrily confronted him, "Father is critically ill, I have taken care of him and your family and whatever is left of our land. We live a hand to mouth existence; there is poverty and despair all around and you are running away yet again."

"So, what do you expect? I too join you with the begging bowl."

"No; but when you came back I was filled with hope that the two of us would and could have worked towards better tomorrow. At this hour when I need you the most; you are leaving me in a lurch.

When I was alone I longed for you

When we are along you want to walk alone"

"I was rightly advised of not to go back as India is full of gloom, hopeless and self pitying people always clutching on others to swim them to the shore."

"So who are you if not an Indian?"

"I am a NRI and soon to be a British citizen".

Sandeep was gloating, so Swaraj reminded him, "Therefore you are showing so much airs, but you have misconception about your worth."

Sandeep interrupted, "No, brother it is you who are mistaken, you always stayed good, always remained hopeful and helpful and it got you nowhere, you are struck where you were and I have become the king of my destiny. And why do you long for my companionship, when you have your dear Siraj. Let me go."

His pernicious behavior and every word shattered his heart into pieces. He saw no reason of playing music in front of deaf bull, as Sandeep had already made up his mind. The last thing he wanted was to be burdened with caring for a joint family. He wanted to live life to the fullest without any responsibilities.

Sandeep shrugged Swaraj off. He caught Rukmini's hand and began to drag her out of the house. Rukmini was unaware of Sandeep's plans. Her thoughts were muddled, they were coming to her in a deluge - if I leave with Sandeep, then I will be deserting my world, my village and above all my family who has given so much care and love in his absence. If I stay I will be a burden to my poverty-stricken in-laws, I will be breaking the laws of marriage that compels me to support all my husband's decision, what about Rohan's future? Is this a passing storm? Will everything settle down with time........

Her thoughts were lurking on the edge of the fence, jumping from one end to another and before her inner voice could make judgment Sandeep had dragged her out of the house. She followed him quietly, submissively and without protest.

He disowned all relations to the point of no return. Lying on his bed, Kisna watched the drama unfold in front of his eyes. His eyes reflected his disapproval with 'I had told you so' resignation.

Swaraj was heart-broken and miserable. The only silver lining was that the stain of being his brother's murderer had been washed away. Otherwise he would have had to live his life with the stigma of being his brother's killer.

His last words to Sandeep as he left were "Do what you desire but remember -

'TIME – CHANGES'.

10

Once in Britain, Sandeep with Rukmini and Rohan went to Mr. Williams home. Rukmini had never stepped out of her village but in the past few months everything changed for her: location, climate, people, language, clothes, food, culture, pace of life, surroundings and add to that she had lost her family, relatives, village and country. Her world had gone topsy-turvy. She was a reluctant participant in her husband's scheme.

Mr. Williams was delighted to see Sandeep back. He had heard all about his family member's names; but Sandeep formally introduced them to him, "Sir, this is my wife Rukmini and son Rohan." waving his hands towards them.

Rukmini bowed, smiled and greeted Mr. Williams with a Namaste. Mr. Williams grinned, "Welcome to your new home! You are going to be British citizens in due course, so it's time to change your names. Your new names are Mini and Roman." Looking at Sandeep, he said, "I think the name Sandy will suit you better as I all the time call you Sand-deep because of my atrocious pronunciation."

He continued to grin broadly. "I hope you like your new names."

Sandeep smiled back, "As you wish Sir your wish is our command."

First she had lost her identity now it was her name too. Unaware at Rukmini's disquiet, Sandeep jokingly explained "The British when confronted with tongue twisting names change them to their liking" citing the example of Bambai as Bombay, The reference that she could easily understand.

Mr. Williams was quite amused at the connection that Sandeep had employed to explain their name change policy. It appeared to him as more of an accusation rather than an honest explanation, so he quickly intervened, "Hey, hey Sandeep, Don't blame us for the name change, we just twitched the name of 'Bombahia', the name that the Portuguese gave it and it became Bombay."

"No Sir, I didn't mean to offend; I don't know the history about its origins. It was only once that I visited a temple named Mumbadevi in Mumbai and over there I was apprised with its name and connection to Bombay. In-fact we in our village call it Bambai very similar to..... What you said? I forgot. What the Portuguese said it?"

"It was 'Bambahia' it means a 'Good-Bay'. Now tell me what's wrong if Bambai is called Bombay. The name has a zing of modernity".

"And it sounds pleasant to the ear" added Sandeep.

"Ok, enough with your name game. Now go and change, have a rest and make yourself comfortable".

The whole communication between Mr. Williams and Sandeep took place in English. Rukmini watched wide-eyed and dumb, shuttling her eyes from Sandeep to Mr. Williams and back. Sandeep deliberately engaged in an argument with Mr. Williams in order to impress upon Rukmini his hold on the language and to make clear to her that this kind of change he meant and intended to bring to their lives.

As promised Mr. Williams took his family to the immigration centre and completed the formalities to make them naturalized citizens. Thus Sandeep officially became Sandy.

The entry of women changed the atmosphere in the house of males. From now onwards Sandy and Mini divided the work between them. Sandy gleefully accepted all outdoor activities like gardening, attending to visitors, purchasing groceries, vegetables, provisions from departmental stores, driving Mr. Williams around and left Mini confined to the villa. She willed her time in tasking all indoor chores: cleaning, dusting, cooking and washing.

Some months passed, with Mini's presence in the house, Mr. Williams began to nurture a feeling for Mini; she aroused in him a feeling of lust. He began to follow her around and secretly eyed her sultry, voluptuous body, toned curves, her walk, her supple movements. He lustily gaped at her exposed midriff, navel and flat belly. Her spangled blouse formed round breast shape that would titillate his senses. Her transparent sari would reveal her lifted cleavage, particularly when she would bend or bow to clean something. Once or twice their eyes would meet and she would squirm and adjust her sari. She would see a different Mr. Williams ogling at her, she thought she should mention Sir's strange behavior to Sandeep, but knew that he would not believe that Mr. William would covet her. Instead she preferred silence and pretended to be engrossed in her work.

Mr. Williams began to stay at home and kept Sandy, who was unaware of his motive, busy with all outdoor activities.

One day Rukmini had finished her bath. She stood at the edge of her room's door in petticoat and blouse and left her sari on the bed. She had knotted her hair in a bun and wrapped it with the towel, droplets of water cascaded down her cheeks and bare back. Her blouse had damp patches and as she unwrapped her hair to wring and dry. Her wet hair sprinkled drops of water on her body like beads. Her body shined like polished wood. Her figure enticed with scintillating sensuousness. She in her prime of youth sparkled under the mild sunshine.

Up, above and from behind the folds of curtains Mr. Williams watched enamored. His desire for sexual intimacy reached its pinnacle.

One day he purposefully sent Sandy out of town, feigning some urgent work to take advantage of his absence. Mr. Williams cognizant of meek surrender approached Mini. He stealthily reached Mini and groped her from behind. She was terrified when she saw him and as he had expected she begged helplessness. Mr. Williams snatched the end of her sari and unrolled it from her body, she crossed her arms over her blouse but he tussled with her on the bed and thrust himself on top of her and tried to fondle her breasts.

Sandy had missed his train. He had a spare key to the house and when he unlocked the door to his room. He saw Mr. Williams trying to assault his wife. To Williams bad luck his plan failed by Sandy's unexpected arrival.

Mr. Williams was perched on top of Rukmini and she was shaking him off her body. Sandy boiled with rage and in the heat of the moment he lifted the suitcase in his hand and smashed it on Mr. Williams head with ferocity.

Williams was hit fatally, the blood oozed out of the wound and dripped on his clothes. He felt dizzy, stumbled and sprawled on the floor.

The injury was so serious that Mr. Williams needed to be hospitalized. But he refrained from registering a complaint and instead said that the wound was due to an accidental fall. He didn't want his reputation to suffer. But more important, he felt deep remorse for what he had done.

Mr. Williams had always been a benign, tenderhearted, mature and level-headed person but his one moment of insanity proved costly for him. He regretted his blunder so deeply that his jaw-line started to droop, wrinkles appeared on his face overnight and he became weak and infirm, unable to resurrect; soon he was confined to his bed.

As Mr. Williams condition began to worsen. His only wish was to atone for his mistake. To this end he made a life changing decision regarding Sandy. He called his lawyer and changed his will. His earlier beneficiary was the Confederacy of Nuns, but now Sandy was the recipient of his largesse. He pledged all his wealth and worldly assets to Sandy.

Sandy could have been arrested for injuring and assaulting. He could have lost all the goodwill that he had earned for years. His job could have been lost. He could have been sentenced. But, instead, he was showered with wealth. He would be the owner of his estate, shares and money. The fateful event turned his bane into boon.

Mr. Williams had no legal heir or close relatives, only few distant relatives with whom he had little to do with. Sandy by default or because of Mr. Williams fault would be bequeathed with all his wealth and property after his demise.

Sandy had by now forgotten his anger, forgiven Mini and absolved Mr. Williams. He began to look after Mr. Williams once again as if he was his father. Never ever sparing a thought for his real father whom he had left back home to die a slow death.

But, Mr. Williams continued to linger on with life, cheating death in his bid to stay alive, his medical expenses were exorbitant and it slowly started eating into his savings; which Sandy now regarded as 'HIS' money. Sandeep's frustration increased

'When would his life change?' He would question himself.

Mr. Williams existence was futile, how long would it carry on like this. So one day he decided to end it once and for all.

He smothered Mr. Williams to death in his sleep.

This was his second felony, the second life he had taken in his path towards betterment. And both time he impelled with the logic that he had put the tormented souls to rest and hence he was innocent of the crime.

Sandy and his family had been in Britain for three years. Mr. Williams was gone and he had had another son. By the time of his second son, Sandeep had become the owner of William villa, the birth of his second son proved lucky for Sandy and so he named him Lucky.

11

✦

It was year 1975.

After Sandeep had came back, stayed and had returned to London, forever. The men were back in Bombay after the monsoon break. But somehow work at the port had slackened and became a bit irregular much to the frustration of the porters. Now they had more idle time then work. They were unable to fathom out the reason for slackness.

One day Siraj and Swaraj were sitting on their haunches, forearms rested on their knees, fingers clasped and backs leaning against the walls. Both were lost in thoughts, looking aimlessly at the sea as if searching for some lost drop in the ocean.

Breaking the silence Siraj softly questioned "Do you have any news about Sandeep?"

Swaraj shook his head.

Siraj continued "You know that I abhor Sandeep. I always knew him to be secretive but I never expected him to stoop to such a level, to run away from his responsibilities.

He could have helped to take care of your father and the family; to me he his despicable". Then digressing from his tirade he said "His behavior is like our neighboring country any amount of goodwill you shower on it or treat it like younger brother, it always backfires." Swaraj listened unheedingly "He is a silent assassin, a back stabber."

Swaraj finally replied, "Yes, his silence was like a dormant volcano waiting to erupt. I didn't take his wandering about on his own as a sign of things to come." He sighed in disgust "He was a man of few words, his silence betrayed us. Words convey feelings; words define characters and thoughtful words wisdom."

Siraj shot back "Sandeep had none, perhaps he spoke little because he was a small person, characterless. And few words are not sufficient to judge a person's sagacity."

Swaraj didn't like his remark but he knew Siraj always spoke his mind and had no ill feelings. Swaraj appreciated his friendship.

Swaraj seemed to be in the mood to confide in Siraj. He continued, "I've always liked reading. We both work at the port, but I like to observe each and every ship when they anchor as well as when they sail away. I am fascinated by people, their attitude, their mannerisms, their friendliness, their carefree casualness and their eagerness to know about our country, our culture, our way of life. I have an urge to see their world the same way as they come to see ours. I envy Sandeep only because he is enjoying his life in the new world, a better world, first world, the world that I want to explore. Today I'll tell you one more secret I always carry with me a small pocket-sized notebook to write down information about the country that catches my attention; and a map of the world to mark the destinations I wish to visit if possibly in my lifetime. The land of the Arabs, Africa, China and the West" he smiled and said "And land of all human species and specimens that frequent our port. This is my unfulfilled dream."

Siraj listened to him in bewilderment. It was first time if he could recollect correctly that Swaraj had been so confiding, and so expressive. He said "Good to know that selfless humans can be envious and desire something for themselves."

Swaraj stood up lazily, shook Siraj playfully, then stretched out his hand to help him stand up and end the chat for the day as it was soon going to be dusk and another day had passed by without much work.

***

The gloomy monsoon was over, leaving India engulfed in the political turmoil of the Emergency.

Work at the port was dwindling with alarming regularity. All the workers were dependent on ships and they of late had been coming in one's or two's or after a long wait.

Another day went by with no work Swaraj and his group was huddled in a circle trying to understand this slump.

Pheku asked "What is this Apatkal; that we have heard so much about these days and they say it has been implemented in our country? Is this affecting our work?"

Another added "I had learned in school about bhootkal, vartamankal, bhavishyakal and even akal but what is this new disease called apatkal?

Nawab said pointing towards Swaraj "Hey mister all-knowing, please shed a light on it".

Swaraj rued, "What to tell you friends, the ships are not coming on top of that my newspaper sales have gone down, this emergency has muted many newspapers and have rendered me without much work".

Nawab again bothered "You read it in papers, share a bit of your wisdom, dear".

Swaraj as usual explained, "Once when I visited a hospital and as I was dawdling along the corridors I saw the word Emergency written on a door".

The others interjected "Yes, we had seen it too."

"I stopped a hospital attendant and asked what the word meant. He explained that the door leads into the Emergency ward where people who are in a critical condition and need urgent medical attention are taken."

"Ok, now what has the word Emergency written on the door of a ward; has to do with Emergency in India. Why don't you directly come to the point instead of going round and round in circles." someone grumbled.

By that time the manager had come strolling around and joined the discussion.

Pheku chided "Stop whining, everyone over here are not as smart as you are to understand directly. We need detailed explanation."

Nawab hushed everyone "And for the sake of others please co-operate, Swaraj has his way of explaining so that each one of us can grasp the matter." He signaled Swaraj to continue.

"Whatever information that I have snatched from hearsay, from the newspapers and discussions with the manager sahib. I had summed up that our country's democracy had been stabbed badly by autocrats. It had been beaten up severely by censoring media and disallowing lawful assembling. It had been comatose by misrule and according to the authoritative powers of the government. It has been declared that there is internal threat to the nation and hence there is a need for emergency. The name purposely or unintentionally is befitting the situation. Our country is indeed in an Emergency."

The press had been prohibited from misreporting, so all we hear these days are glowing accounts of the governments achievements. All unions are banned".

Nawab jumped at the mention of union and asked the manager "Sahib, where is our union leader?"

"I also don't know he went to his village and has not returned as yet"

"He is always the first to return than what may have happened?"

"As he fights for your cause he has many cases registered against him with the police; he may have got the whiff that this union business will get him in trouble and so he has not returned. But, good for me, he will no longer gherao and create a nuisance by his nonsense demands and disrupt the port functioning." Said the manager as he went away, before going he cautioned them to end their meeting quickly.

Swaraj continued "Exactly this is what I was saying. Anyone can be arrested without any rhyme or reason without any crime or treason. It all depends on the whims and fancies of the authorities."

"Our country is the patient and we, the people, are the harried lot." He paused.

"Ok, ok I think we have understood enough about the Emergency."

"The reason for our slow work is the current political environment."

"It is the culprit."

"Who would be interested to come to invest on a dying person, or in this case, the country?" One of them asked in a dejected tone.

Everyone had an opinion about Emergency.

As the manager had ordered and just as they began to disperse, Swaraj fired a parting shot, "Beware young men, don't get caught by family planning officials, touts and doctors. These days sterilization is the latest racket."

"They are on the hunt to trip the flow from your tool that reproduces." Siraj winked and made a gesture with his two fingers to suggest snipping off the testicles.

This last bit of whisper made their ears stand tall, they stopped in their tracks. They wanted to know more about this new clause since it affected them directly; so all over again they continued to discuss and it went late into the evening.

Manager on his second round saw them still deep in discussion. He clapped his hands and scolded, "Why the hell are you still sitting in a circle? The times are bad. You all could be picked up for unlawful assembly and conspiring against the government and so a threat to internal security."

"But we are under an enclosed area."

"Don't forget dock is a public place and they have power to raid without warrant and with all of you they would arrest me as well, as I am in-charge of all of you."

"On, what charge?"

"For planning a rebellion"

"But we are not planning anything. You can deny"

"That's the whole point. I can deny. But I would be without a chance to prove until Emergency is in place."

"Is really our country under internal threat?"

"No, it is under individual threat. There is no need to panic only be a little cautious. No more questions, now move" the manager called for the final time.

Till this time they had taken this phase of political turmoil lightly but manager's firm words made them feel that the situation was actually very grim. They got up, upset, as they finally dispersed.

The policemen's visit to the port and slums to collect their weekly bribe ceased abruptly. The slums along the shore and around the port were demolished and some areas were spruced up under the city's beautification program. The slumlords went underground or fled away. The people that would gather enmasse at short notices to display their ire or block demolitions were lathi-charged or hurled into police vans and were dislocated to far-away places under the mantra of 'Garibi Hatao' which really meant 'Garib Hatao'.

The corruption and black-marketing were controlled; files that had gathered dust were unearthed and passed tables swiftly and smoothly. Government offices and transport facilities worked punctually. At the same time, freedom of speech and freedom of press, the two strong pillars of democracy were strangled and squashed. There were some good points and some bad points that came out with the implications of Emergency.

12

✳

They had got adjusted to new pattern of work under constant fear as they had become union-less, now they didn't have the union leader to take up their matter with the manager, without a leader they were forced to be self-disciplined. They had recently talked about Emergency; Siraj had recently joked regarding sterilization campaign. And he became the butt of his own joke. The effects of Emergency walked straight into his family. One evening as Swaraj was waiting for Siraj at a place where they daily had their dinner. He saw him come huffing and puffing towards him, with an urgency that denoted that something grave had happened.

Siraj was holding his elder brother Mehraj's arm pleading to him and pulling him towards where Swaraj was seated. Mehraj had run away to Bombay to evade forceful vasectomy.

Mehraj already had six children, four boys and two girls and there was really no reason to produce anymore. Siraj and his whole family had tried many times before; they reminded him of his fallacious beliefs. They were enervated by their efforts. He was under the influence of religious doctrine and was stubborn to listen to anybody. Now that he had come to Bombay, Siraj with a hope that Swaraj's wizardry with words could convince Mehraj to have change of heart; as a last resort he brought him to Swaraj and explained the whole matter.

Mehraj was like Swaraj's elder brother and he addressed him with respect. Before speaking Swaraj took a long pause and began, "Ok, then brother, why do you want to increase the numbers of your offspring when you have more then you need, in fact, more then you can afford."

Mehraj replied, "It is God's wish. Don't you know 'God gives, man receives'". He shook his head in disgust at Swaraj's lack of understanding of such simple logic.

"Ha, valid answer, but then doesn't God wish many more compliances from you."

"How does this make sense to our discussion?"

Swaraj knew that Mehraj was a tough nut to crack so he explained patiently, "Do you pray regularly abstain from all sins or obey all God's commands without question?"

Mehraj meekly said "No."

Taking this as his cue, Swaraj replied "Then follow all God's commands whole-heartedly, not just those that suit you. Or make an exception to this one also as you do so with all his other wishes."

Mehraj, spellbound for a while, gathered his wit to retort "Doesn't God guarantee the survival of a new born?"

"Agreed, God is the provider, he will provide for the food, he will not let us sleep hungry this is what he has promised and this is what your holy book says. Am I right?" questioned Swaraj.

But it is the bare minimum, the other aspect of the new born is what we have to look after, we have to give him good clothes, good education and a better standard of living. We have to guarantee them a safe and secure future in this high demand world."

He elaborated with an example, "Suppose that a house has a family of four and that a couple of them are earning members and the others are dependents. You will notice that they have high or satisfactory standard of living. But if that house is filled with eight people and only two are working and the amount of income is the same, the standard of living goes down drastically because there are more dependants. This is the truth in your case."

Mehraj silently absorbed what Swaraj had said. Even though he accepted his reasoning; he still held pride in his logic and not to go down without a fight. He fired a barrage of questions, "Who gives the government the right to decide how many children a person should have? Is this the right way to control population? Are you lecturing me because you support the Emergency?" Saying so he stood up agitated.

Swaraj calmed him down by requesting him to sit down, "My, brother, no political or ruling system is without flaws, every coin has two sides, every decision has multiple consequences and multiple perspectives. I personally think population control is one of the best decisions taken during Emergency."

"For the sake of nation sometimes hard decisions need to be taken."

"Reproduction beyond requirement is always a burden and a nation of unwanted populace is a thrust on its limited resources."

"The manager once explained me, it was written in English daily 'DENSITY' and 'DESTINY' have interchangeable spellings. In India's context density will be largely responsible for shaping India's destiny which means that population will severely affect India's future."

"If we want to secure our children's future we should act now."

Swaraj's impassioned debate had by now impacted Mehraj's sentiments. Siraj was awed by the way that Swaraj has turned Mehraj's feeling of victimization to one of responsibility towards the country. At the same time he had convinced Mehraj about the disadvantages of having too many sons.

Mehraj knew that he would not be able to wriggle out of political compulsions and though not truly convinced of Swaraj's advice yet he acquiesced to undergo vasectomy.

***

The next day was a very eventful one for Swaraj. He was on his own because Siraj had taken the day off to take his brother to the railway station.

Swaraj's old towel had frayed and shredded so he replaced it with a new towel, on his shoulder. The towel was not a decorative accessory instead it served multiple purposes such as to wipe the sweat from the face and arms, a head-wrap as protection against the scorching sun and as a cushion between the head and luggage.

A huge ship had arrived late in the evening and as usual the porters began unloading the luggage. Swaraj carried a lady's suitcase to the car park. She was a beautiful, English lady wearing a long white frock printed with red and pink flowers and high heeled sandals. She wore a baby pink pearl bracelet on her slender wrist and big beads pearl necklace and held a purse dangling on her forearm; she wore a breezy light perfume and a large hat. The lady was on a business-cum-pleasure tour. She was a jewelry designer by profession and had brought samples of her designs to display in a trade fair in order to find prospective buyers and customers.

The ship was late to the port by some hours so she was late for an appointment. She opened her purse to pay Swaraj for his services and as she hurriedly rummaged through her belongings to find the money, her vanity case popped out unnoticed and fell down.

At the same moment Swaraj's towel also slipped and dropped to the ground, covering it completely. The lady hastily paid him, flagged a cab and jumped into a cab. Swaraj took his time to count the notes, touched it to his forehead, kissed it, then kept it in his pockets, and then when he knelt down to pick up his towel, he found the vanity case, but when he looked around, the lady had disappeared.

It was late and the lost and found office at the port had closed, so Swaraj took the box with him to deposit it in the morning. Out of curiosity he opened it and was startled to find that it was filled with precious stones, necklaces, diamond rings, gold jewellery and gold biscuits. The box was like a pocket size dynamo whose effect could change any person's life. This put him in a dilemma.

A scene from a Hindi movie unfolded before his eyes in which two facets of a person's character confront one another- one guiding him to sanity whereas the other incites him to fall into temptation and commit a crime.

The evil one allured him by reasoning:

* The Ship had hordes of passengers, all alien faces are alike; how will you recognize the owner?

* The vanity box is in your possession. The lady doesn't know where she has lost it and even if she recollects where she might have dropped her box, she cannot accuse you; and even if she does you can flatly deny having seen any box.

* Just imagine what its worth is. It can change your life and put an end to all your miseries.

The reasoning of the evil side had the conviction to make him succumb, and all the while the good side was keeping him firm rooted to his honesty.

Swaraj tossed and turned in his bed restlessly for the whole night, unable to sleep. Finally he woke Siraj up in the middle of the night and disclosed everything to him. Dislodging the weight off his chest, he went to sleep peacefully.

Still it was some hours from the dawn. Siraj got up quietly from his quilt and tip-toed towards Swaraj's trunk. He opened the trunk and took out the case. He quickly surveyed around then tucked it inside his shirt and began to run. The clatter woke Swaraj up and he shouted his name. Without turning he ran as fast as he could. Swaraj chased him; he held him by the collar and tried to stop him. He saw rage in Siraj's blood-shot eyes. They both had a fight and in an ensuing fight Siraj picked up a stone and rammed it onto Swaraj's head. Swaraj screeched and fell down; and with it Siraj woke up from his nightmare with a scream.

His scream woke Swaraj and he saw Siraj's face drenched in sweat. Swaraj asked, "Are you alright?"

Siraj repeated the same question, "Are you alright?"

"Why are you asking me? It was your shout that alerted me out of my sleep."

Siraj touched all over Swaraj's face to assure that he was safe; he hugged him and again repeated "Are you alright?"

He stayed still for a while then understood that it was a bad dream. He replayed his dream and said, "This wealth is a very evil thing, it can shake the faith of the strongest willed person."

Swaraj said, "I am not a saint. I was also a bit squeamish. I too had to control my instincts that veered towards unscrupulousness. You are not to be blamed and you should not carry the feeling of guilt, we are poor people so we are easily susceptible to cheat and so we have the two fold responsibility to show our integrity. The first thing we'll do is hand over the treasure to the manager."

Siraj agreed and said, "Swaraj you are a gentlemen, I am proud of your decision."

Early next morning Siraj and he went to the manager's office. The lady by then had discovered that the case was missing and was in his office to report her loss. When she saw Swaraj with her bag she was relieved. She thanked him gratefully and checked if all her belonging were intact. The manager introduced Swaraj to the lady, endorsing his honesty. She marveled at the honesty of this poor porter and as a token of her appreciation, presented him a gold coin, encased in a jewelry box with her name and address embossed on top. At first Swaraj refused to accept it, but Siraj nudged and persuaded him to do so. He bowed before the lady, thanked her and hesitatingly accepted the coin.

Luck had finally smiled upon him. He deposited the coin with the manager for safe keeping and when he returned to the village, he opened a locker in the bank and stored away to use it in a time of crisis.

13

❄

Swaraj at last heaved a sigh of relief that for now all his troubles were at rest, for a time being he exhilarated in the air of comfort unaware of a new trouble that awaited him.

A faint shadow of a lady in distress appeared in the verandah on a dark and wet night. It was pouring cats and dogs. Her face was speckled with water. The sari was fully soaked with water trickling down from the edges and she held a bawling little girl in her tow. It was hard to differentiate between raindrops and teardrops. Was rain falling on tears or tears falling down as rain?

Outside it was pitch dark and it was raining heavily. Swaraj picked up a lantern in one hand and an umbrella in another and went to have a look at the mysterious figure that had appeared in his verandah at an odd hour.

To his dismay, it was Nirmala standing, looking heavily pregnant with Shrishti by her side. She had reached wading her way valiantly through the gusty winds and inclement downpour. She had been ousted of her house with nothing except her daughter.

News of Nirmala's divorce hit him like a thunderbolt. Both Devi and Swaraj were in a state of shock, unable to react. They would often visit Nirmala but she never seemed to have a turbulent marriage. She always turned up to be lively and contented. They were never aware of the storm brewing in their backyard. They looked at each other and by grasping the gravity of the situation, they hurriedly went towards Nirmala and open heartedly welcomed her in the house.

Kisna also came to know about Nirmala's return. This was the last straw that broke the camel's back. Kisna was no longer able to take it anymore. He suffered a major stroke and passed away. There was grief and despair in the house.

Swaraj was unprepared for the sudden unexpected expenses. His savings were negligible and not enough to bear the cost of the funeral and other condolence ceremonies; besides there was now Nirmala and her daughter to take care of.

Bad fate befell upon him as soon as good time had knocked on his door. The gold coin as a gift by a compassionate lady passenger didn't stay long with Swaraj. He closed his bank account even before it was truly activated. He sold the gold coin but retained the jewellery case as a souvenir.

Siraj felt sorry for Swaraj and took back his words of wisdom on destiny for Swaraj's continued bad luck and accepted god's verdict. In his silent prayers he hoped for the best for Swaraj because he knew for sure that he was the good man who had always been caught in bad situations.

Swaraj performed his father's last rites and after a stay of few days returned to Bombay.

Nirmala was in her last month of pregnancy; she went into labour and delivered a still born female child.

Devi and Nirmala had known each other since they were children; they were classmates as well so they addressed each other by names. Nirmala was a sincere, obedient, helpful and trustworthy person who always appeared to be carrying the weight of other people's problems on her shoulders. As a result she appeared very thin and weary. She had one exceptional quality; she never confided her troubles to anyone, she kept her sorrows to herself. Devi was quite sure that Nirmala could do no wrong and the fault lay with her husband and his family.

Although she wanted to she could not muster up the courage to ask Nirmala as to what went wrong without them knowing? Why she concealed her wretched marriage? She gave Nirmala time to settle down after the trauma of divorce. She knew that the truth will be known one day, so she never pestered her to divulge her side of story.

In due course Nirmala adjusted herself back in her brother's home. Devi and Nirmala involved themselves in the household chores. Nirmala was very hardworking and more than helpful to Devi. Devi felt blessed for having a sister-in-law like Nirmala.

One day out of a blue, Nirmala's grief filled to the brim, unable to control her emotions anymore. She broke down in front of Devi and narrated her ordeal.

She began, "After the marriage when I went to my in-laws house all was hunky dory. My in-laws specially my husband would take great care of me and fulfill all my wishes even without me even asking for it. Until one day when I got pregnant. I was jubilant even my mother-in-law was ecstatic. She would go around the town telling everyone that Nirmala is pregnant and would certainly deliver a baby boy. She would keep cajoling me to give birth to a baby boy as if it was something under my control." Devi listened attentively, nodding in between in approval.

"Shrishti was born and that was that" she said flinging her hands downwards. "All the love and affection showered on me ceased at once, they were not ready to accept Shrishti. In fact they were so allured at the prospect of having a male child that they accused the hospital staff of changing babies, they knew the truth but they were ready to raise another person's child as theirs, only because it was a boy" she paused "I was agitated, frustrated but unable to fight back in this bizarre charade of inhuman behavior. However when they were left with no option they accepted Shrishti." With a knot in her throat she continued "The next time I was pregnant, my in-laws took me to the hospital for a sex determination test and with the connivance of the doctors they were able to determine the gender, to my bad luck it was another girl and they forcefully made me have an abortion." Devi got lugubrious at Nirmala's fate.

Nirmala sniveled and wiped her running nose with the edge of her sari. "Two years passed by and the third time I got pregnant, I delayed them the news in the hope of saving my child. But my baby bump, had started to show, my in-laws took me to the hospital. Alas the result was the same, but luckily the doctors refused to abort citing medical reasons that the time for abortion had lapsed and now it was too late. I felt fortunate to have saved my baby girl." At this Devi exulted, but her joy was short lived as Nirmala continued. "My mother-in-law started to taunt me by saying how large hearted they had been to allow their son to marry me without taking a dowry, but what would happen to my daughters whom I was giving birth to one after another." She looked helpless. "As if I was the culprit and their son the sufferer.

My mother-in-law would say, investing in girls was like storing water in a strainer always futile and waste of money.

I always protested vehemently, the rebel in me would confront. I would angrily say 'If everybody thought that way you and I would not be here today. She would silence me by saying 'the proficiency to debate does not change the reality of the circumstances' I could have argued forever but always conceded defeat owing to the culture of respect for elders that is imbibed into us."

"The mental torture began endless. They began depriving me of nutritious food and not enough food to feel contented, they rationed my food supply, when my daughter was born she was severely malnourished and emaciated, not to live long in this cruel world."

Devi dolorously commiserated with Nirmala, nevertheless in awe that she never said a word to them when they visited her at the hospital, at the same time she was disappointed that if she had revealed they would have known and would have perhaps sorted out a solution.

But it was not the end of her terrible tale. Nirmala continued in desperation "The last time I was pregnant. I hid my pregnancy by wearing loose clothes till as long as I could but how long can a bulging belly belie the news, as soon as it was known. I had to go through the same routine and the result was same. The doctors indicated that if they went ahead with the operation both the child and the mother could die. To my horror they were ready to take the risk just to get rid of a girl child even to the extent of sacrificing me. I was amazed at their blind desire for a male child. My husband as always was a mute spectator. The mental agony now started to get physical. I could have taken it for as long as I could, I didn't wanted to add to my brother's burden but I had no place else to go. I adjured they abjured and the harrowing became unbearable but before I could take any initiative action, I was thrown out of my house." Nirmala said with tears rolling down her cheeks.

Devi lachrymosely heard Nirmala plight, pointing at the nearly defunct transistor radio that Swaraj had brought back on one of his visits, she said sadly with clods in her voice, "On the radio we hear a lot about Indra Gandhi being the strong lady, for me you are the real strong lady. You did your best to save the gender you belonged to. You are the pride of women hood. I pity the mother in laws who being women themselves shun women and baby girls." She paused for a while and then reasoned. "May be it is the evil of dowry that makes them remorseless and unrepentant." Wiping off her tears she said "Let bygones be bygones, start your life afresh, make yourself comfortable and stay as long as you please, this is your house." These words filled Nirmala with assurances.

Devi knew that Nirmala was a brilliant student, so she suggested "Why don't you start studying again, that way you will be Independent." Nirmala wanted to unburden as well as share her brother's responsibilities, but was hesitant because she feared the society for calling her names that she would be at fault or might be she wanted to be independent and so she left her in-laws to pursue her dreams without anybody knowing the true story, the gossip mills would start churning rumours that are baseless. Besides that she had left her studies long time ago so would it be fruitful to go back to it again?

Devi encouraged Nirmala with thoughtful words, "Let anybody say whatever they want you must have belief in yourself and your ability. God, is the only one you are answerable to, secondly when you know that you are not wrong then why fear about other people's judgement and thirdly when you rise its morning, the saying that is so very well said, so it's better late than never." Devi gave Nirmala more than one reason to think over, Nirmala ruminated over Devi's suggestion and agreed to study further.

She helped Devi with the household chores and became a teacher in elementary school to support her studies. She burnt the midnight oil in her resolution to succeed.

Nirmala sat for her Bachelor of Education entrance exams and was selected for the course in the nearby city. She left Shrishti under Devi's care and went to city.

***

The house was in shambles because of unaffordability for repairs. Devi had made it in a livable condition with some changes in the interior of the house with whatever scrapped furniture they possessed. They was an iron bed with stinking quilts and ragged, frayed, soppy bedding because of years of unending use by Kisna, the pillows were filled by rag clothes, the tattered clothes were stored in two-three tin suitcases that served as closets. In the kitchen the wood stove was replaced by kerosene stove, there was still no sign of electricity with lantern as a source of light. Mostly the house would be in dark after dusk. The exterior was excruciating asking for repairs with moldering walls with chunks of mud crumbling in heaps.

Arun and Shrishti were playing on the verandah as Devi grumbled looking at the plight of her house. She babbled animatedly to both about the house; being children, they neither were able to understand nor were they interested as they were busy with their childish games.

Devi sat there and watched them play for a while before she retreated to the kitchen to cook.

After she left a postman called from the gate. Generally, the postman would visit the house at the beginning of the month with the money orders from Bombay but for him to come with an odd letter at any other time was a rarity. He always came with an open 25 paise letter but never with sealed envelope and that too with an envelope emanating a hypnotizing fragrance, so Arun excitedly questioned him, "Whose letter?"

The Postman said, "Don't know" but he added with a glee in his eyes "It's from some foreign country." Arun fetched the letter and ran into the house.

Arun gave the letter to Devi who opened the envelope to read it.

Sandy or say old days Sandeep had a premonition, a certain tick of blood-ties that he had some days back called up for his father at the village post office to enquire about his well being. The post master had conveyed him the sad news of his father's demise.

So Sandy after mulling over it for few days, after giving it a long drawn thought; after weighing the consequences; after sulking at an illusionary belief of him being neglected under favoritism and shadowy existence of Swaraj; after steely determination of wiping his slate clear of his past; after a resolve of snapping old ties. He wrote a venomously worded condolence letter.

Brother Swaraj,

I am saddened to hear about the demise of our beloved father. I pay you my condolences and regret my absence.

You must be thinking that I am a traitor to have ditched my family and home for greener pastures. But I have also endured a lot of difficulties. You must have thought of my life as a bed of roses, but I have crossed many hurdles, uncertainty, fear, adjustments issues, buggery, slavery, comprising with religious beliefs and honor. Finally I have reached a level of respectability.

I want to stay where I have reached and I do not want any partner in it. I would be unable to share any of your family's liability as I have my own problems and my own family to look after.

In-fact father passing away must be happy news for you as it has absolved you of his onerous existence.

Coming to the point, I am uninterested in his property; I permit you to keep my share as I no longer intend to return to you or to your life. I also hope that you too do not induce any hope from my side. This is probably our last communication. Thanks for understanding what my reasons are.

Yours Brother,
Sandeep

She was shocked to read the content and tone of the letter. The words of condolence were just a formality; he actually intended to sever all ties with Swaraj, now that Kisna was no longer alive.

Devi was livid. She didn't want Swaraj to agonize about his brother's vindictiveness, so with a twig on her face she cursed Sandeep in her breath then she crumpled the letter and threw it away.

Arun watched the turn of expression on his mother's face, he couldn't understand what it meant but had the inkling that this letter had some importance. After she left he gathered the crumpled letter. It was addressed from someone by the name of 'Sandy Keeshun Goswamy' and the address was '52, William Villa, London, Harrow, H A-2, 1 BA, United Kingdom.'

Arun instinctively smoothed the creases that had appeared due to the crumpiness. He pressed the envelope flat and tucked it into the back cover of 'BhagwadGita' that was always placed on the ledge below the idol of the deity in the small temple in their living room.

Nirmala was studying for her B.Ed. At the same time she gave tutorials, worked part time as a baby sitter job and stitched clothes. She multi-tasked and got busy in life. She had started to earn enough to take care of herself and Shrishti. She rented a room in the city and took Shrishti along with her - in the process she took her first step towards independence.

Arun who was exceptional at studies was an apple of his teachers' eyes. The principal would vouch for his brilliance. He envisioned a bright future for him and suggested to Swaraj to send him to the city school which had hostel facilities. The village school would help financially and arrange for a scholarship. Thus Arun started to study in the city school.

14

Meanwhile Sandy was overjoyed by how his luck had changed and the windfall he had inherited. He thought to himself 'What's the use of being a master, if you don't have a servant to look after you'. So he began his search for a Butler-cum-servant to replace him, someone who could perform all the tasks that he once did for Mr. Williams. And he found one.

He had toiled all his life and so he treated his new help with compassion, not taking advantage or exploiting him. For the first time he displayed his humanitarian side.

He would gloat to himself, 'From being a servant in William Villa I have become its blue-blooded master.'

He chose to retain the name of the property as William Villa since it sounded very English.

He had wealth, now he carved for social status. He started inviting people from the neighborhood for social gatherings. It was an exclusive suburb of London, inhabited by the upper crust. He had tried his best to fit into English society by attempting to imitate their mannerisms, he put in his best efforts but failed miserably. He was not accepted whole-heartedly.

He decided to reinvent himself. Having and needing to do no work he begun to take lessons in etiquette. Being with Mr. Williams had helped him understand and speak English, but he now wanted to polish the flow and accent.

Mr. Williams had left Sandy so much that even if he spent extravagantly it would last for a long time.

It was the irony of excess, the person who earned it had lived a frugal life but now his wealth was being splurged by someone who was not even remotely related to him, such is the travesty of life.

Sandy dejected by snub was silently swallowing his pride and by that time the borough of Harrow transformed itself from a sedate English suburb into the home of rich Indian expatriates. They were dynamic entrepreneurs cashing in on the benefits that the foreign land offered and were making their presence felt.

The main road towards his villa were now lined up with shops selling authentic Indian wares, clothes, temple offerings, books, magazines, novels and all kinds of regional literature, music stores blared out Bollywood and Tollywood songs, movie theatres show-cased huge cut-out of stars, Indian groceries, Indian restaurants and Indian coffee shops and snack parlours. It all created an aura of mini India.

Sandy began to feel at home with these familiar people, he felt confident and returned to his partying ways - sort of beginning his second innings. Because he was the oldest inhabitant and assumed to be the richest because of the sheer size of his mansion, he started getting invited to his neighbor's homes.

Mini resented the party culture. She was a reserved homemaker unlike Sandy who blew money away like bubbles. She had endured days of hardships and so she would always nag Sandy to occupy himself with some work otherwise all this unnecessary expenditure would make him a pauper one day. Sandy thought her a buffoon and her advice nonsensical.

With time she was able to speak pidgin English. Sandy hired a tutor to make her speak fluently and she achieved eloquence with course of time. He also made her discard her saris for western wear as well as encouraged her to change her ways. Being a dependent and obedient wife Mini unwillingly hosted and accompanied Sandy to parties. She adapted herself with aplomb and transformed her appearance to match Sandy's.

The new neighbors knew nothing about Sandy's past. They had assumed that he was a self made man. Sandy presented himself as a successful stoke broker with investment in stock as his business. To show off his expertise, he would pass tips on shares of which he had elementary knowledge, but he said them with such confidence that he was believed.

At parties Sandy would freely mingle with everyone but didn't like Mini talking to any men. Here his Indian male chauvinist attitude would rear its ugly head. He would eavesdrop on Mini's conversations and after every party he would quarrel with her on some issue or the other. The fissures in their relationship started to widen.

At one such party at Sandy's house, Sandy was in the house looking after arrangements and entertaining the guests while Mini was standing at the entrance receiving the guests. A handsome guy appeared at the door. Mini being a courteous host greeted him with a smile. He on seeing an unknown host realized his mistake that he was at a wrong address and said, "Sorry."

Mini smiled again and to guide him to the right address, she craned her neck and pointed at the distant house and while doing so she lost her footing and tumbled. The guy held her hand and averted her from falling. She quickly got back on her feet, jerked and smiled shyly. He smiled back apologized again and left.

Sandy saw this from a distance and as he had become a doubting Thomas, this irrelevant incident was enough to poison their relationship. A trivial non issue led to irreconcilable differences.

That night Sandy and Mini had a heated altercation. Sandy enquired, "You always complain that you don't like these social gatherings, then what was so special today, that made you so extra courteous towards this guy?"

Unable to understand his point, Mini asked, "Being a host it is my duty to welcome all my guests with a smile, so who was it to whom I was so courteous that it had pinched your heart?"

Sandy replied, "The one who held your hand and caught you by your back and to the one in whose arm you swayed."

Mini guessed his undue concern and snapped back, "This is just your devious mind trying to start a quarrel."

Sandy was infuriated at Mini's answering back and in the heat of the moment, he said, "It was for my son that I came back to India to get you. I would never have returned if you were alone. You should be thankful to me that you are enjoying the luxurious life you could never ever have dreamt of. It is my mistake and it can't be rectified. I allowed you to dance on my head."

His words broke Mini's heart. This spark engulfed their married life. Their relationship had reached an irreconcilable juncture.

Mini spoke for the final time, "OK, I am giving you a chance to rectify your mistake, give me divorce, that way you will get your freedom and I will return to India".

Sandy seemed as if he was waiting for such a situation to arise so without a second thought he promptly agreed.

Mini was uncompromising on leaving her sons behind but due to influence of culture and coercion by Sandy, her own sons turned back on her, the influence of foreign culture was more dominant than her motherhood. She didn't desire to go back to her village or relatives but to Bombay city. She was ashamed of going back to her village, to relatives whom she had reluctantly renounced due to being a servile Indian wife.

It was the year 1985, when Roman was fourteen and Lucky was eight that Mini and Sandy got divorced and parted ways.

After the divorce Sandy felt liberated. He became a party animal. Socializing was his favorite pastime. He would take Roman and Lucky along with him to every party. Lucky would get along with girls of his age and would always be in their company whereas Roman would remain aloof. Sandy would observe both his sons behavior and would encourage Roman to be like Lucky. After every party Sandy would taunt Roman that he was like a timid Indian lad by not accepting the British way of life. Fed up with continuous prodding at parties and taunting at home Roman decided to change himself with a vengeance.

He was good looking and smart. He started body building and transformed himself from a lanky to a tall muscular guy, sparkling like a polished diamond from a rough piece of stone. He dropped all his inhabitations, his flamboyance attracted girls and gradually he too started to like the attention. He had become the latest heartthrob.

One of their neighbors was a girl called Shanty Shah, the daughter of rich Gujarati family. The first time she saw Roman, she had developed a crush on him. She was drawn by his coyness. She had observed his transformation from a shy guy into a Casanova. His shyness attracted her, his boldness capitulated her.

With time, her infatuation turned into unconditional love and every time, she saw Roman her heart would pop out but the words of expression didn't. She couldn't muster enough courage to pour out her feeling to him, more so since he was always surrounded by girls. He never even glanced at her, even though he knew she existed.

Sandy's second innings at the party circuit garnered him some white friends. His network of influential people expanded. At one such party, he was introduced to a girl named Sarah Parker. She had all the flouncy airs of a temptress - long free flowing blonde tresses, angelic face;

pouted lips a la Jolie, curvaceous body. She was wearing a resplendent red gown and her only accessories were red earrings and sandals. Dark red lipstick complimented her milky complexion. His heart skipped a beat when he saw her. He was floored by her beauty and vivacity. His heart started to hum the song 'Lal chadi maidan khadi.........................hum dil se gaye, hum jaan se gaye bas aankh ladi aur baat badi'

She continuously flirted with her hair that fell over her face. Her flirtatious charm intentionally clamored for attention. Her beguiling glance would make strong minded men bow before her in submission. She had a killer look and everything to a tee, everything to die for. Sarah was impressed by Sandy's extravagance she was updated about Sandy's financial status and recently attended bachelorhood through her circle of friends. Sarah's roving; almond-shaped eyes had surveyed the room and hunted its prey. Her eyes zeroed in on Sandy. Sandy was to be her man.

Sandy was hooked up by Sarah instantly. Soon their casual meetings ended in serious relationship. They bumped into each other at parties and the relationship bloomed. Sandy proposed and Sarah accepted. They got married.

Soon after marriage Sarah began to show her true colors. Rumors about her past started to emerge; Sandy began to scratch deep into her history and the deeper he dug the more he was shocked; the murkier her past emerged. Sarah in her past life had been an escort, a floozy girl who would eye rich and powerful men, lay a trap and hook them, play with their emotions and laugh her way to the bank. Her provocative way of carrying herself, her mesmerizing and contagious smile, it was a masquerade. Sandy realized that he had been trapped.

Sarah was a gold digger and her real reasons for getting married were to extract huge alimonies from the divorces. To that end, she would target the vulnerable.

The honeymoon period was short lived. Sarah with her battery of high class lawyers squeezed the maximum alimony from Sandy. For the first time in his life he was heart-broken. He got the taste of his own medicine.

Most of the priceless paintings, Monalisa that adorned the centre wall of the hall, some cars, diamonds, shares and cash were given as alimony. His prodigal ways, the two divorce settlements, particularly the second one, had stung him badly. Divorce settlement depleted his fortunes severely. He became a drunkard.

William Villa had a long history of being averse to female presence; denying female to stay in it for long periods.

Mr. Williams had purchased it when he had returned from India. His wife had lived with him in India; they had a happy married life but as soon as they moved back. She felt her wings clipped, stifled within the confines of the huge estate, boredom had set in and she yearned for freedom and gained it with a divorce.

His second wife was a free high flying bird not to be caged within the boundaries of the villa. She launched into a even higher flight and eloped with a younger and sturdier aviator to flutter her wings around the world.

Mr. Williams lost interest in the institution of marriage. Instead he decided to confer the title deed of William Villa to the Confederacy of Nuns. The house that could not bear the presence of one woman would have become the home of many. But circumstances had nipped his plans in the bud.

Sandy had brought Mini here. She had been the longest resident of the Villa, maybe allowed to reside because she stayed in the outhouse longer than in the house.

Then came Sarah Parker for a brief stay.

Monalisa an iconic portrait of femininity too was unceremoniously snatched from its prominent wall hanging.

With the addition of Butler now it was an all male house again.

Denial to female presence was probably a curse of William Villa.

Roman, in the meantime, following his father's footsteps had overtaken him by many steps. He too became a party animal, moving from one party to another, further denting Sandy's finances. The parties of the younger generation were filled with booze and sex. One-night stands were common. In order to increase his libido he started taking sexual enhancing drugs. His profligate lifestyle started to affect his academically as well. From being an excellent student his grades fell. Lucky, on the other hand, hung out with only a handful of friends, a mix of both sexes.

15

❇

Swaraj's youth almost passed away working at the port. Years of toiling had taken its toll. Age had caught up with porters even before they grew old. Some had become bandy-legged, some bald, some hunchbacked, some retired exhausted by the heavy workload, while some died prematurely from diseases like tuberculosis, dengue or malaria, some even caught Aids due to reckless night-outs, and very few from Swaraj's batch remained trudging along enduringly.

Swaraj's physical appearance had changed as well, but his financial state remained the same. The only glimmer of hope for a better future was his son Arun.

Arun was an excellent student, and by 1989, he had completed his high school and was preparing himself for college admission. His field of interest was Computer Science, a new vocation with great career opportunities.

Between 1989 and 1992, India had witnessed three major political events. These three years changed the dynamics of the country as well as impacted Arun's life to a great extent.

Arun's grades were very high and he had applied for admission to a top notch Bombay College. Unfortunately he could not make it on merit as he had missed out by one percentage point and the seat went to a student under reserved category, even though his percentage was lower in comparison.

Arun felt cheated. He was unable to digest the criteria for selection and the commotion this sudden change in the selection procedure had created to his career. He felt like a casualty of appeasement politics. His only option was admission on the payment seat but not on merit.

When Swaraj came to know that Arun had missed out on admission and the vague reason for it, he felt melancholy. He told Siraj "Do you remember many years back, one day I told you about upliftment. That day I was happy for the downtrodden but today it has come haunting me.

Have you seen in any game there are two sets of rule for two teams?

A tougher challenge for a stronger team and an easier challenge for a weaker team;

"No that's not the case" Swaraj self answered "Even the underdog have to perform, beat the better team, winnings does not come on a platter. We all feel pity for the weaker team but we do not change the rule in their favour to make easy for them to compete. They have to prove that they have the ability.

In reality the performance had been dismal but the gains for them have multiplied because of patronage of political class."

Siraj knew that Swaraj was depressed for Arun, after all the hard work he had missed out on admission, it was so near yet so far case for Arun, but as usual he was battered by Swaraj's verbosity. As usual, he was unable to understand the context of his talk. Swaraj continued, "The standard of education is being compromised for the sake of lifting the standard of the population. The criteria for selection should be financial position and not caste one is born into." After venting his anger, Swaraj calmed down and explained Siraj what he actually meant.

Now that he understood the problem, Siraj remarked, "This should make us the most suitable candidate for upliftment, but here we can't change the situation so we must learn to adjust to it. Adjustment is what is expected from voiceless people like us." He observed before adding, "This kind of reservation gives advantage to the undeserving."

Swaraj was so disturbed by the events that he had lost track of current events and so when he heard that a certain boy named Goswami had immolated himself to protest against the Mandal recommendations, his heart sank. He ran to the manager's office to confirm the news. He rummaged through the old newspapers and discovered that the boy was not Arun Goswami.

Manager Sahib had grown wiser over the years. "In the days of British Raj the lower classes wanted to climb the ladder to reach equality at all cost. But now after forty-three years of Indian Raj, the trend has reversed. Now to gain the benefits, they are all in a hurry to climb down the same steps that helped them reach a semblance of equality.

And the best part of this reservation business is that even the well-off are dying to be tagged as underprivileged.

This is how fortune fluctuates, sometimes thriving for being called better; sometimes striving to be called worse." He said in a prudent tone.

Swaraj consoled himself that it was fortunate that Arun had got selected on payment seat. Now it was up to him to arrange funds to pay for the fees.

Swaraj found himself in the same position as Kisna whenever he had financial difficulties. The land which had provided them status and livelihood had once again became their only asset in time of crisis. After being in Bombay for years, Swaraj had little contact with village life.

Babulal had accumulated large tracts of land but he still eyed Swaraj's piece of land as it was holding in the way of his ambitious farmhouse project; Babulal had special interest in Swaraj's land as it was on the outskirts of the village and an ideal location for his nefarious and pleasure activities.

Babulal was patiently waiting for Swaraj to buckle under the pressure of need for money and come begging to purchase his remaining piece of land. Swaraj too knew that the only door that could answer his call was of Babulal and the circumstances dragged him on the path of Babu's door.

Swaraj had decided to sell off his entire land and house and shift to Bombay after Arun finished his studies in four years time. Thus he entered into a mutual agreement with Babu that after four years he would hand over possession of his land and in exchange Babu will provide the fee money every year in installments.

He thus became landless investing in Arun's future.

Swaraj had told Arun about how Manager Sahib had explained him the reservation confusion with the example of a ladder. Arun got inspired with the idea and decided to prepare a drama using the ladder as a metaphor. Arun with studies actively participated in dramas. He used the stage to put forward his point of view. He directed and performed in a skit with the help of his fellow students.

The play began:

Scene 1

A foreigner with his Indian friend is strolling in the garden. They stop to watch the children play.

Ring-a, ring-a roses
A bucket full of postings
I want I want
And we all fall down.

But some remain standing. Those who remain standing are declared 'Out' by those who have fallen down. They shout, "Out, out, disqualified, disqualified."

The standing ones defend themselves, "Why should we be out? We are standing; we didn't fall, so those who fell should be out."

The fallen ones reply, "Didn't you hear the rhymes? It says that the one who wants the postings must fall."

"The lyrics are wrong. How can you win if you fall? To win you have to stand against all odds, to fall means to fail, how the one who fails be declared as winner." They argue.

"It is the rule of the game. If you want to qualify, you have to fall!"

"These rules are very confusing, if you do not change the rules we are not playing." They protest.

The standing ones refuse to accept the verdict. The fallen ones refuse to relent. They start to debate and fight.

The foreigner looks mysteriously at his friend. His friend just coolly smiles back without saying a word and they move ahead to reach another part of the garden where they watch another group playing another game.

Scene 2

There is a ladder that leads to the platform. On the platform there are few seats. The platform has a board with words 'DESERVED' written on it. There are some brilliant and well dressed children already seated on the top seats.

There are many seats at the bottom too; those bottom seats are also occupied. The seats at the bottom around the ladder also have a board with words 'RESERVED' written on it.

In between, there are lots of children standing on the ladder. They have nowhere to go. The children on the top are firmly holding to their seats while those on the grounds are filling the space and claiming even the vacant spots. Stranded children on the ladder instead of climbing the ladder upwards are trying to climb down the ladder. They want to climb to the top but are unable as over there the space is crunched with very few seats and held by the one who deserved it. They see some vacant space on the bottom and are left with no option then to climb down and fit into that space. They are desperate to the point that they are ready to dive down to gain the slot.

The children on the down warn them sternly, "Don't eye these vacant spaces. You are not going to get them. They are our seats."

"We can see there are some empty spaces." They shout.

"They are for our brethren. You won't get it."

"We will dive and capture the vacant seats."

"Don't you dare to dive; we are sitting with rocks in our hands. Don't expect pity if you get injured. Remain where you are."

The foreigner is confounded at the absurdity of this unusual game.

He questions, "I agree that the ones who have reached the top are the obvious winners. But how can someone who has made an effort to climb are left stranded and how come those on the ground do end up as gainers.

I am crazed, 'Why the children on the stairs are not interested in climbing up but are hell bent on jumping down, why they are not competing to win?"

"They know that winning is improbable so they are taking shortcuts."

He asked impatiently, "Who made all this silly laws?"

"These laws were good when they were initiated. They were set for a time frame to see the results. These laws were enacted to give power to those who were on the ground as the children on the ground are weak and they should also get the fair chance to compete."

"But now they are acting smart, aren't they?"

"Yes now they have become obstinate and are flexing their muscles by not allowing the change in law."

"Why are they so stubborn?"

The Indian friend says to the foreigner, "You come with me to the bus stand and I will show you how seats are captured over there. It is if you drop your handkerchief or keep your belonging on the seat it gets reserved as your seat. Over here they have reserved seats and who is the fool to let go his seat."

The friend takes him further to the third scene to show him the final skit.

Scene 3

Here the children are playing a drama. The place is a License making office.

The officer asks an applicant, "What is your name?"

Applicant, "Ramanujan"

The officer scratches his head then writes down, 'Ram Manjan'

The applicant gets angry and spells out his name R A M A N U J A N. He then goes and sits in the corner sulking till he is called back.

On another cabin, the second officer, "Your name please"

Applicant, "Fatima"

He writes down 'Pratima'

"Sir it is Fatima, haven't you heard this name before.

He looks blankly at her. She too spells out her name.

Ramanujan and Fatima are seated next to each other, they began to berate the officers and guffaw at their inaptitude.

The foreigner is unable to understand the children's weird game and its logic.

He asks amusedly, "And what about this third act."

The friend looks towards the audience and says

"This third act is the derivation of the first two games. It is the work pool that the country produces because of its policies. The ones who occupy the top seats play hard and with sheer determination and when they get the chance they change the garden and go to foreign gardens over there they know that they have a level playing field. And they know that if they stay in the same garden they will again get harassed and the same problem will arise at their next level.

The foreigner shakes his head at the mediocrity of the reservation laws and the play ends.

***

With this the curtains came down and the hall erupted with claps.

The curtains of the play went down but the curtain of controversy unfurled. The opinions were divided. The play gained accolades from the affected and brickbats from the targeted. The drama hall was vandalized.

The college disciplinary members liked his idea but were apprehensive about appreciating it and they were forced to condemn it. They called Arun into the office to keep his point.

One professor questioned him, "Why did you delve upon such a contentious issue?

"To bring to the fore the flaws and its impact on the fundamental rights of equality for all its citizens"

"What difference can a play make rather than open up the can of worms."

"It was my try to put sense into nonsense in the name of reservation. I agree that they are deprived; they need to be treated at par. But it should be done at grass root level. If they are not allowed to plough their fields, if the bridegroom is not allowed to ride on the horse on his wedding day, if they are barred from drawing water from the community well, if they are restricted entry into temples, if the police do not note down their complaints, if they are abused, threatened or beaten. These are the issues that need their help. The more heinous crimes that take place are ignored and shielded. Education is made the scapegoat. Education is made the poster boy to show equality. But in reality this system snatches the seat of the deserving student. In the name of equality it is injustice."

"Our country when it got its constitution was declared the 'Republic' but it should have been called 'Reservation Republic' because that is what we have reduced ourselves to. This fire of reservation is going to remain kindled and will remain a tool to stay in power. This will be a trump card that will sweep all other issues of development and divide the people as us and them. The elections are fought on the basis of which caste holds how much percentage of votes in the constituency and not on local problems. This will remain a blot on the country that would never be cleaned as it serves the purpose of those in power.

The professors asked him, "You have raised an issue. It is easy to protest but can you provide a solution"

"Yes sir" he said.

And they got eager to hear him out.

He questioned, "Why can't we have 50% reservation for women?"

"How will it solve this menace?"

"It will solve all the problems related to reservation. It will give reservation to half of the population of the country. The benefits will be accrued to all. It will help control female infanticide. It will help to reduce the imbalance of male-female ratio. Moreover it will end appeasement of any particular caste. No caste or religion will feel vindictive."

The professors heard him patiently then declared, "You are free to hold your views, you may be correct with your assessment, but you choose a wrong platform. If you would have raised any issues pertaining to the evils of the society, it would have been acceptable. This is a college auditorium and not an open ground, where you can raise your agenda. We do not support any ideologies. We do not want any controversies on our premises. We want a written apology and a promise letter that you will not delve into such topics in future. We are leaving you with a warning this time. But next time you will be rusticated."

Arun silently admitted his mistake and submitted an apology letter.

As he came out of the office he saw a waiting crowd of supporters with garlands in hands, a cheering group of students. He was hailed as a hero. He was looked upon as a future leader. He was coerced to fight for their cause.

In coming days he was approached by representatives from political parties, all extending their support and willing to give him ticket to fight campus elections.

Arun had played with fire, he had raised the issue but he was reluctant to ride the horse that he couldn't control. He felt like he had been thrown into a coliseum to fight a tiger. He was amazed that his skit could create such an impression and make some of them so impassioned.

He went to his father for advice. Swaraj by then had come to know about Arun's growing fame as a youth leader.

He said to Arun, "I have heard you are preparing for college elections."

"I am compelled to fight, what should I do Baba?"

"Student politics is a stepping-stone into a full-fledged political career. And politics is a muck that will suck you into it. Politics is a quicksand pond, the more you try to clean it the more it pulls you into it. You will become dirty but politics won't get clean. People enter politics with a slogan that they want to serve the people, but politics is for those who have nothing worthy to give to the society. Politics is the business in which lot is promised and little is delivered. Politics give power and power corrupts. Politics is for corrupt, shame-proof, conscious-less and stone-hearted and you are none. I don't want you to get involved with it.

If you have any aspirations to live a rich and powerful life, I would request you to instead, live an honest and respectable life. For that concentrate on your studies, you are a bright boy. Get good grades and settle in life and leave the unworthy to take care of politics."

Arun went back to the college and surrendered his nomination papers. He joined his palms, downed his eyes, shook his head and said sorry to all those who had pinned their hopes on him, to those who wanted to see him as their leader, to those who backed him, to those who pushed him on the forefront and to those whom he had disappointed. He quietly steered himself clear from all the hoopla and hibernated from campuses political activities.

16

Came the year 1991; in that year the government took a very wise and reformist decision to liberalize the economy and end the License Raj. This opened the doors to multinationals and competition by transforming the economy from manufacture controlled to consumer oriented.

There was a buzz in Arun's college campus with discussions between students on the effect of this resolution.

The faculties explained during lectures that MNC's will be able to do business in India, liquidity would increase through Foreign Direct Investment and job opportunities would grow. There would be cut-throat competition among manufacturers leading to better products with competitive pricing that would benefit the consumers. The overall market and infrastructure will improve. This was one of the best resolutions passed by Independent India. Time will judge its impact.

These words sounded like tinkling bells in the ears of Arun and his co-students. This was the golden period for young India.

Liberalization was a soothing balm that had helped Arun to forget the pain of the Mandal Commission like a bad dream. Now he looked forward to the twinkling prospects of a bright future.

Due to limited means Arun lived in the cubby-holed, chaotic and filthy slum city of Dharavi, in the heart of Bombay. Living chock-a-block with people all over, he had made friends in the neighborhood.

Arun was fully aware of the hardships his father had to go through to educate him and so to earn some pocket money he started working in an electronic device-making unit in the slums after college.

The electronic unit that Arun worked for made inferior products but charged high rates. They were devoid of competition and used second-hand, run-down and depreciated machinery, paid minimum wages and employed under skilled labors, lacked technical know-how, but were sheltered under License Raj.

With liberalization and arrival of foreign products in bulk, entry of multinationals and better pricing; the local manufacturers were unable to withstand the onslaught of heavyweight competitors. They started to feel the heat; the sales plummeted, inventories stock-piled, losses increased and lay-offs began, Arun was one of the casualties of the lay-offs, his services were terminated and in due course the units closed down.

Arun's first experience of liberalization was a setback, instead of blessing it turned out to be a curse for him.

He questioned his professor, "You had shown us the golden dream of prosperous India with the policy of opening up of the economy. But the local companies are closing down and due to it I got unemployed."

The professor heard him out and then explained "When a season changes from autumn to spring. The old leaves wither away and make way for new leaves. The new leaves give new life and fresh fruits to the tree. The rudimentary mentality of closed economy had stagnated our growth. With the collapse of the old structure of License Raj, the new leaves of liberalization will blossom and the tree will bore fresh fruits. This would be the new leaf in our progress."

Arun remained idle for a short period; he was devoid of any job, so to supplement his income he started tutoring local neighborhood kids. His daily routine had begun to settle was when the disruption occurred.

The political pendulum again struck him the wrong way. At the fag-end of 1992, turmoil hit India. The Babri mosque was demolished and riots erupted.

Anarchy prevailed over peace, divisive politics over unity and brotherhood, hatred over love, betrayal over trust, madness over sanity and cruelty over humanity. Suddenly friends turned foes, ghettoization became the buzzword and Arun was caught in the melee.

For the first time since he came to Dharavi, he felt insecure living in a minority-dominated ghetto. The neighbors, who shared every happy and sad occasion with him, started to distance themselves from him. The parents of kids who had addressed him with respect as 'Sir' now abhorred his presence.

One night, a volley of rocks and soda bottles filled with the venom of hatred came pelting down the rooftops of scattered Hindu homes, the specifically targeted ones. There was total panic, as people ran here and there to save themselves and their kith and kin, shrieked with fear.

There was fear all around –fear of being a cast-out, fear of the dark night, fear of fellow humans, fear of intensity of hatred and the fear of death loomed large. All kinds of fear mashed the minds of few Hindus within a Muslim stronghold.

Cries of 'Kill, Kill'

'Infidels Infidels'

'Tit for Tat'

'They are killing our people by thousands let us kill some hundreds'

'They have clamped curfew in our areas leaving them free to plunder murder and rape.'

There was shouting and chaos, threats and abuses, stone pelting and street fights.

Riots demarcated the areas and souls into us and them.

The slogans that praised God 'Allah-o-Akbar' and 'Jai Shri Ram' had become a war cry. The horror of riots rang loud and clear and instilled fear.

The lanes that Arun knew at the back of his hands were deserted into long alleys, the door that remained always open were shut on the face.

A neighbor, a boy named Aftab, also meaning sun, came to Arun's rescue. He took Arun home and took care of him by sharing his room with him, comforting him and offering whatever food he could afford.

Arun wanted to make a distress call to Swaraj to let him know that he was safe. Communication reforms in India were still some years away; the STD booths and local PCO's were doing brisk business. The charges that were usually Rs 2 for an outgoing call had been hiked up to Rs20, while incoming calls cost Rs10. But this call rate only applied to Arun because he was a Hindu. The telephone operator refused Arun the liberty to make a call. Earlier he used to give him credit but now he demanded that he clear the debt first and pay the charge if he wanted to make a call. In this way he took the advantage of the situation as well as spat out his anger.

Arun was penniless, the amount demanded was princely and above all he was out of work because of the riots. He always had limited means and with no savings due to his hand to mouth existence.

Aftab was considerate of Arun's plight but helpless.

Arun and Swaraj were in the same city but were unable to connect. A few miles distance appeared poles apart as there was curfew clamped all around the city. Swaraj was extremely worried about Arun's well being.

He and Siraj were sitting at the port ideally as all work had stopped and they had no other work rather than to sit workless and discuss the present scenario.

Both rued the maniacal situation in the country more so in Bombay, which was considered cosmopolitan and the least communal city in India.

Swaraj dejectedly said, "The majority community should not be suspicious and prejudiced and view minorities as traitors. While the minorities should do away with the perception of being victimized and being treated as second class citizens."

"Riots are the device used by politicians to entice the gullible masses into doing wrong for their political gains."

"If the Mandal Commission was vote bank politics at its worse, then communal riots are vote bank politics at its worst."

"Both communities should rise above minority-majority politics and keep India in their hearts and mind.

The politicians make two religions fight to polarize the elections and gain the prized trophy of the hot seat in the parliament. But once elected as a member, he should work for all and cast aside the affiliations of caste, religion and any other tag attached to his identity, they should represent themselves as Indian.

Divisive politics will ruin and divide the nation. On other hand, development will definitely make India a force to reckon with."

Swaraj like always was eloquent, Siraj like always was enchanted. He had the same thoughts going but didn't know how to put it in words. He nodded in appreciation.

The stillness in the air of December 1992 had an unnerving alienation. The underbellies of ghettos were churning from within and the human divide was palpable. Religion began to be worn on sleeves - Hindus preferred saffron, Muslims favored green and the rooftops unfurled the flags of identification. Cynicism, skepticism, suspicion, distrust all the words related to doubt floated in the eyes of known and unknown. There was an eerie calm before the storm.

A month later, the riots again flared up, the same lunacy repeated itself. Arun who was caught in the vortex for the first time again found himself in the same maze.

Swaraj thought enough is enough. He didn't want Arun to be vulnerable anymore and thought that he would be safe inside the campus in a college hostel even though it would be a further stress on his finances. He took the hard decision of selling his land outright, again at a loss, and move permanently to Bombay. There was nothing left for him in his village.

For the first time in his life Siraj felt the pinch of separation. He never lived away from Swaraj. Swaraj was his guide, mentor, confidante and the most reliable man in crisis. Above all he was his best friend.

Arun shifted into the campus, and Swaraj after putting aside the money required for his fees used the balance amount to rent a ramshackle shack in a slum area. Devi initially found the setting different though not difficult to adjust to. It was neither better nor worse than their ancestral home in the village. More so, it was all Swaraj could afford in exorbitant city like Bombay.

17

❄

It was the summer of 1996. Britain comes to life during summers, like Indians rejoice the arrival of winter as period of relaxation and vacationing. The onset of summer energizes the Brits, they enjoy the most after the harsh winter months.

But the weather made little difference to Sandy. He no more enjoyed partying and social gatherings. He had became a loner and retreated into his shell. Roman and Lucky had grown up and were now out of their shells. Roman had completed his graduation with average grades, and continued to squander on booze and girls. Lucky on the other hand, was studying Fashion Design.

The Indian Butler at their villa; would finish his day's work after adorning the dining table with the dinner menu, leaving it upon them to self-serve. He would retire to his quarter. He refrained from poking his nose or picking up the noise of Sandy's family affairs. They were of no interest to him. The family too didn't want him intruding around. It was an agreement that worked both ways.

Dinner was usually a silent affair. They sat and ate as strangers

But on Lucky's eighteenth birthday, an altercation arose between the three of them. Normally there would have been a party to celebrate the occasion but both Sandy and Roman had forgotten his birthday, one living in seclusion the other in illusion.

This was Lucky's night or perhaps Sandy's doomsday.

Lucky sat on the table, fidgeting with his spoon and fork and ignoring sumptuous, aromatic and piping hot array of dishes laid in front of him.

The clatter disturbed Sandy and he asked, "What's the matter Lucky?"

Lucky was waiting for the cue, "Today I want to make the revelation." Said Lucky

Lucky was an introvert and rarely spoke and for him to start a conversation meant that something serious or extremely important was about to be revealed.

Was Lucky going to pull out a rabbit out of a hat? They thought; amused and sat back in the chairs to keenly listen to his announcement.

Lucky still fidgety, cleared his throat and blurted as his voice clogged his fear, "Have you ever seen a confectioner eating his own sweets?"

Roman with a blank face waggled his fingers and with a soft cackling laugh asked, "What, what absurd question is this?"

"It's a very valid question, if you can answer it"

Roman said "Of course not dear, now will you spill out what your fear is." Lucky's hesitancy and fidgeting had alerted Roman.

Lucky asked again earnestly, "Why?" He was trying their patience in a bid to buy time to confess to what he thought was his crime.

The food was cooling down, the conversation was heating up.

Roman ruffled at his nonsensical questions and growled, "Are we playing some sort of a quiz. You are asking questions so obviously the answers as well as the explanations should come from you." He banged his spoon with a thud to make Lucky aware of his mounting frustration.

Lucky again responded in a roundabout manner, "Anything that is available easily and in aplenty loses its value for the one who has it and at the same time it is valuable for the deprived as he carves for it. A confectioner loses the desire for the tempting sweets in his store because he can have it whenever he wants. He becomes saturated to the desire to have his own sweets."

The conversation was now reduced to the debate between the two brothers with Sandy as a silent spectator. He never spoke a word.

Still not able to understand the point Lucky was trying to make Roman scolded, "What are you trying to say? Your conversation is going round in circles, and now even I am confused. Are you fearful that you chose a wrong career path of Fashion Design and now you have realized that you wanted to be a confectioner? Are you thinking of venturing into sweet making business?" he smirked.

Lucky not to prolong this any further as this was his golden chance. He disclosed, "This example is best suited to me."

By now Roman had completely lost his cool and seething his teeth, he asked, "How?"

"From childhood I was exposed to the opposite gender and I liked to mingle with them. It was not because I liked them but because I felt comfortable with them. I liked to have male friends but not as chums or pals. I was attracted towards guys."

Roman still maintaining his calm asked, "Than how is it that you didn't make us suspicious, even for an iota of a second, that there was something effeminate in your personality."

"I was coward and ashamed of myself and therefore pretended to be manly. I was not true to myself."

Roman swallowed his anger and remarked calmly, "You are still a young man to know the consequences of your revelation."

"I am not complaining that you forgot" said Lucky with a dramatized pause and continued "But today it's my eighteen birthday, and it has been a very hard and calculated decision to reveal my sexual orientation to both of you."

Roman till now holding back his anger with super human effort finally lost his cool and snarled, "Idiot, it was to compete with you that I transformed from good to bad and worse, but you remained a step ahead and turned from bad to worse to worst".

"Did I ever ask you to compete with me?"

"No, it was dad."

Lucky shrugged his shoulders and pointing with his chin towards Sandy commented, "Then why are you accusing me? Father is responsible for what you are today and you have no right to blame me. Father is infact responsible for what I am today"

His last quote perplexed Roman as to how father was responsible for Lucky, while Sandy's face wore an impassive look by not reacting to the accusation.

Roman retorted, "Your revelation will besmirch us. It's a bad small world. Here gossip travels faster than genuine news, disgrace faster than fame, scandal faster than morality. Your revelation has all the spice to whet the appetites of the gossipmongers."

"Those who live in glass houses should not throw stones."

Roman found this comment tough to digest, as he knew it was directed at him.

There was no stopping then. Allegations and counter allegations between the two brothers flew thick and fast. The conversation that had started as a quiet family dinner exploded from a tiff into a full blown quarrel. Roman and Lucky began to shout on top of their voices.

The charm with which they had began to hear about the revelation suddenly turned into harm of reputation.

The quietness and tranquility of the neighborhood was shattered by the verbal volley. The butler peeked from his window to inquire about the ruckus in the Goswamy household but decided not to intervene in what he thought was a personal matter.

Lucky walked off in a huff. Roman felt nauseous and retired towards his room muttering and shaking his head in disgust.

Sandy was flabbergasted to respond and had sat at the table static and speechless as the drama unfolded in front of him. He was too numb to react.

Different setting, same scene and years apart, it was like a recreation of the past when he and his brother quarreled and their father had watched helplessly.

Next morning Roman woke up late. The previous night's altercation had been forgotten and he went to Lucky's room to reconcile.

Lucky was not in his room. Roman thought Lucky would have left early. But at night again at the dining table when Lucky didn't appear that Roman and Sandy felt something was amiss. They searched for him in various places, checked with his friends and acquaintances but Lucky was untraceable.

Roman called in the cops. The police started their investigation. They searched the entire locality and during routine questioning, they stumbled upon the Butler's version of the previous night's altercation between two brothers, of the ruckus in the house sounds of clanking utensils and raised voices.

He revealed, "At first, I was concerned about the noise, the Sir and the babalogs are a quiet lot and they eat their dinner as if they are in a mourning, hardly any sound is made, hardly any noise is heard and hardly any voice is raised so the dinner table drama kept me awake for the whole night. I couldn't sleep and stayed seated by the side of the window ledge. I saw a ghostly figure coming out of the house, he had a cap on his head and he was dragging a big case. The brothers have the same physique, so I am not sure who of the two it was. He went past the main gate and disappeared. This was all I was able to see from the distance, in the dark moonless night and in the feeble light of the hanging bulb."

Going through all sources of information such as personal diaries, the computer, and friends' version, and after a thorough interrogation of Roman, they came to know the reason for the fight between the brothers. Cops coincided and combined the events to conclude that it could be a case of honor killing, and detained Roman on suspicion.

Sandy knew that Roman was falsely implicated, but as of now all the fingers pointed towards Roman and Sandy had no way to disprove it. Instead the cops warned him that he was also 'a person of interest' as a co-conspirator and instigator.

This was for the first time that Sandy understood the trauma his brother Swaraj must have faced when he disappeared and felt sorry for Siraj as he now realized for how he would have felt for being falsely implicated into the crime he didn't have a speck of knowledge about.

In prison, Roman had enough time for introspection. He pondered about his debauched lifestyle and decided to reform himself and lead a reputable life hence-forth.

Sandy tried all his might to get Roman released. Again he thought of being in his father's shoes and for the first time he felt truly ashamed of himself.

Roman's legal costs were spiraling out of control, whereas Sandy's fortune dwindled sharply.

After six months, one day out of blue, Sandy received a call from Lucky. He angrily asked, "Where are you?"

"I am in USA"

"What the heck are you doing in the USA?"

Lucky was surprised by his father's hostile response. He was oblivious of the sequence of events that took place after his departure.

Lucky detailed the tale of his traverse

"After that eventful night and subsequent high voltage drama, I felt that my presence would be a blemish on your reputation. I had a secret boyfriend who is a USA citizen. We both were in a long-term relationship and I wanted to spend the rest of our lives as partners. But as same sex marriage is illegal in UK and only legal in Maine, we decided to get registered for marriage in the USA. Our liaison would have been unacceptable to you and so I decided to sneak to America. After completing all the formalities of registering as a couple we are getting married. I am calling you for the last time."

Sandy was ambivalent about Lucky's call, happy that he was alive, but sad because of the reason for the call. He cooled down and narrated the entire incident that took place after his disappearance. He also assured him that he wouldn't interfere in his life.

But he should have interfered when Lucky was an adolescent.

Lucky was not a born gay, the chance incident made one. Some years back at one of the parties he had attended with Sandy, a teenager had taken fancy to Lucky and had seduced him. When Lucky had complained to Sandy, Sandy for once had roared in rage and took Lucky to identify the culprit. But as soon as he saw the accused, he lost his will to fight; he buckled under the weight of his opponent status. Instead of mentioning about the indecent approach he preferred sweeping the matter under the carpet, he silenced him because the teenager was the son of an influential British Diplomat.

Lucky had asked, "Why didn't you show the gut to teach that rascal a lesson."

Sandy hushed him up, "Don't ever discuss the issue again, and treat it like a bad dream and move-on. It would be better for us."

Sandy was improvident of the consequences and in his incognizance he unintentionally sacrificed Lucky's manhood.

Sandy overlooked it as a one-off incident and Lucky never ever complained. He moved on but not with his life instead he moved on towards the guy who had molested him, then he too began to enjoy the pleasures.

As the years passed, the love bloomed between Lucky and the teenager. And after sometime with his father's posting to US, he moved to the US.

But when Lucky called and made him aware of his partner the incident came flushing back to Sandy's memory. Still, why cry over spilt milk? Being in Britain for so many years had made him more tolerant about homosexuality and freedom of choice.

He requested Lucky to personally appear before the court of law to verify that he was alive and thereby prove Roman's innocence so that he could be released.

Lucky agreed but stated that this would be his last visit and he would never return to UK again.

Lucky testified before the court and Roman was acquitted. They hugged outside the court room.

Roman jokingly whispered into Lucky's ear, "When you choose your field of interest as Fashion Design. I had an indication of your inclination. I shrugged my doubts aside but you have proved me right."

Both smiled, patted each other's back. There was no ill feeling nor any love lost between the brothers.

Lucky flew back to the USA with his friend for never to be heard of again.

Roman vowed to start his life afresh. He mended his ways and set out to find a decent job.

During that period, Europe was going through a serious economic depression and in that period of hardship, Sandy bled in stock market and as his only source of income being dealing in shares he lost a fortune. As a result, he mortgaged his villa to help his finances.

Roman was more involved in searching for a job and was rarely around. There was always an imperceptible vacuum in their relationship that had widened.

Sandy became a recluse, rarely venturing out of his villa. He further drowned into the abyss of solitude. All the past events had drained him physically, mentally and financially.

He would spend all his time sitting on the couch at the centre of his large hall. It became his perennial sitting place and the empty wall in front where Monalisa's smile once beamed became the wide screen where he contemplated his past. Scenes of his past life came back to haunt him - his betrayal to his brother, his despicable behavior towards his father, the murders of Yeda Bhai and Mr. Williams and his shrewdness of coming out clean on both occasions, divorcing Mini, his failure in upbringing of his sons, turning a blind eye to Lucky's problem, prodding Roman to change his lifestyle, inculcating a wrong set of values, living in an illusionary world of fragile and impermanent relations, splurging of his wealth.

His only companion was a bottle of alcohol. He was a person of few words but now went into utter silence and appeared forlorn. His idealness made him sick, his disheveled appearance made him look much old than his actual age. Sandy overall was on the verge of bankruptcy.

❈ ❈ ❈

18

✳

Swaraj had now settled in Mumbai, as Bombay had begun to be called. He still worked at port but was on his last lap as he was getting greyer by the day and there was a new breed of younger porters replacing him. As Bombay changed its identity to Mumbai, Swaraj from 'Mukhiya' was now referred to as 'tau' or 'chacha' meaning uncle.

The port too changed its look. With advancement in technology manual labor was minimized and international passenger traffic was diverted towards airports. All these factors meant that there was less need for labor and hence there was downsizing.

Arun finally graduated with flying colors and had many offers from various companies. In the early days of the service sector boom there was a great demands for graduates. Arun remembered the past when he was trying to get selected by a top university, now the trend had been reversed. Suddenly he felt as if beggars have become choosers.

Arun selected a job offer but insisted on a condition. The company was ready to dole out a hefty package of

Rs.900000 per annum, an amount Arun had never seen in his life.

Arun had stipulated, "I am looking forward to working in your company but I want a full year's remuneration in advance and against it I will sign a five year loyalty contract with the company."

Not to miss out on a bright prospect, with high demand for exceptional talent, plus his assurance against attrition, the company readily agreed.

With all that money, the first thing Arun did was to purchase a home. It was year 1994 and the bug of inflation has not hit urban India. The rates were steady and under control, awaiting economic boom and sweeping inflation. The amount was sufficient for Arun to buy an apartment in semi-posh suburbs in Mumbai and Swaraj and Devi shifted into the place that they could really call home.

The household expenses were taken care of by Swaraj as almost all of Arun's first year income had gone into purchasing his house.

After a year when Arun started getting a regular salary he would often purchase electronic appliances and household goods randomly. After three years at the job he had all the necessary appliances, and he then purchased a car on monthly installment on his credit card.

Now that Arun was settled, Swaraj quit his job, making way for younger people to be employed. He told Siraj, "You should also quit while you can. It is only because of our manager's benevolence that we have continued well past our prime."

"Our manager is older than us but he is still continuing with his job than why should we think about retirement?" questioned Siraj.

"Yes dear, you are right, but body gets exhausted much earlier then mind. Body aches but mind doesn't, physical age catches on faster than mental age. Have a look at the game of chess; it is played by big age players and look at physical sports like cricket, hockey or football, they have precocious talent that reaches their retirement by middle-age. In our field of work we are the physical players and our manager is mental player. So don't hang on until you are forced out. Retire and make way for younger porters before the shove comes to a push. Plan your retirement and don't remain uncertain like our sport-persons who are always unsure about when to hang their boots." He said as a matter-of-fact and the advice that Siraj considered seriously.

Swaraj hated sitting idle. They had been in their new home for three years and the neighbors and society members had come to know the Goswami family very well. Swaraj was revered for his good nature, uprightness, honesty. Because of this, he was offered the secretary's post, a post that have remained vacant, as no one was ready to take on the onus of the society's affairs without any benefits. The society selected Swaraj and announced that the post would not be honorary position anymore but a paying service. He was elected unopposed.

Swaraj wanted it to remain that way. He was fiercely independent. He would say my name is Swaraj so he was not dependent on Arun for his expenses. The new job was unexpected, and it looked as if his fortunes were changing. The cycle of time had started its circle. Swaraj's day of reckoning had came knocking.

Arun was enjoying his life, though Swaraj had observed that Arun had become more extravagant with his living style.

One day Swaraj gave him a list of things he wanted to be brought from the market. Arun obliged. He brought everything in excess. Swaraj was out of his wits and he asked Arun, "What is the reason for such generosity in purchase."

Arun replied, "No worry, Baba it's all on my credit card and where the heck do I have to pay for them right now. I am earning well and bit of excess does not matter."

Swaraj thought Arun needs a lesson in responsibility.

One lazy Sunday morning, when Devi had gone to the temple as was her every day routine. Swaraj decided to have a candid chat with Arun.

He was sitting at the dining table pretending to read the newspaper, while Arun was making breakfast.

Swaraj glanced at Arun and called out, "Arun, do you think you are responsible?"

"Of course Baba; as you see I am well settled in my job and life. I am earning well and now own a house. We have all the luxuries, so yes I can say I am a responsible person. Why don't you think so?"

"No I do not agree."

Startled, Arun asked "Why?"

Swaraj explained with the wit and wisdom of an eminent college professor, "You are capable but you are not responsible. Responsibility does not come with how much you can earn, but how much you can save."

The statement jolted Arun. Swaraj continued, "This new world of plastic money is going to make everyone broke."

Arun interrupted "Hey Baba, how do you know about plastic money, I mean about credit card."

"Don't forget that I am a very compulsive reader. I am well aware of the changing world and its activities. So what if I do not use one."

Arun shuts up and listens.

"See this culture of credit money is false. PLASTIC HELPS YOU FLOAT IN DEEP WATERS, BUT PLASTIC MONEY CAN ALSO DROWN YOU IN DEEP DEBTS"

"Never be proud of your position because money has no permanent address. The Arun does not shine always its glare is blurred by the arrival of badal (clouds). If Arun raises so does Arun sets. If Arun shines so does it fades." He exemplified sun to Arun as his name meant the same as sun.

Arun was taken aback by the lecture he received, and sat blankly analyzing what Swaraj had said.

Then the doorbell rang. Arun opened the door and found Siraj uncle at the door.

Arun got a call from his friend and he excused himself and went to meet his friend.

Siraj had bought a box of sweets for Swaraj. They sat on the couch of the living room and chatted for a while then Siraj asked dejectedly, "What is my responsibility towards my brother's family?"

Swaraj was caught off guard by the question and asked him to elaborate on his misery.

"You know that Mehraj has six children, four boys and two girls"

"Hmm, so what?"

"Mehraj's two girls are of marriageable age, but he has exhausted all his resources. Somehow he will arrange for their marriages. They are not the problem. The world thinks that having girls is the only problem but the problem lies elsewhere."

Swaraj perplexedly asked, "Where?"

"As Mehraj was not able to provide and take care of all his children, they remained uneducated and the result is that out of his four sons the eldest one has turned into a hard-core criminal. He is into illegal activities with the police always on his lookout so Mehraj has disowned him. The next one has learned to repair two wheelers and does a job of a mechanic. He looks after himself and provides his bit to the family. The third boy loiters around the whole day. Looking at their plight, I have decided to take care of his youngest son. Now what else can I do to help my brother's family?"

Swaraj pondered for a while as he always did when presented with a query, and then replied, "He has dug his own grave, let him await his fate."

"I had explained to Mehraj during the days of the emergency of the perils of too many mouths to feed with limited means. It's good that he stopped at six otherwise the consequences would have been much worse than what it is. He has created his own problems, now let him find a way out. If a person believes that even if he dives into a well he will be saved, than it is suicide. God created man as the most intelligent animal, with brains, and if he doesn't use them then it's his problem, you need not worry. You have done enough for your brother; now let him fend for himself. You look after your family."

Swaraj's words had the soothing effect of a painkiller that gave temporary relief; it was a short term solution to a never ending problem. Siraj's real concern for sharing his problem was to lighten his heart, seek guidance and find a new angle to look at his worry regarding his responsibilities towards his brother.

By that time Devi returned home and Swaraj jokingly told her, "Today seems to be my day for giving lectures, first to Arun and then to Siraj." Since Devi was absent during that period she was flummoxed, but Swaraj and Siraj had a hearty laugh.

Swaraj then reasoned Siraj, "You were worried, but then you brought a box of sweets. Is it a bribe or fee for my solicitation?"

Siraj grinned and said, "What to do, I have never remained away from you. The reason for the sweets is that I too have shifted to Mumbai permanently as my son had got a job in a vernacular call centre."

Devi asked, "What is the call centre?"

Siraj also expressed his ignorance, "I also don't understand what does he do sitting in an air conditioned office and speaking on the phone and for that he earns the salary that is more than what we earned after a full month's slog."

Swaraj "It is a new job market. It is called the BPO. And it is given the status of a sunshine industry."

Devi gets agitated, "What are you saying? I do not understand a word."

"Then simply understand. They call it a sunshine industry but I call it moon shine industry. The West wake up and does not let us sleep. It is an owl-making industry. It is making Indians owl by keeping them awake all night. It is making Indians owl by paying them peanuts that seems to us as big as walnuts. And they are making the Westerners also owl as they think they are talking to their countrymen but in reality their calls are diverted towards us; Indians."

Devi looked gap-mouthed and Siraj laughed out loud and said, "It is better that we do not understand. Then to ask you and forget what we had asked."

Siraj kept on shaking his head in amusement, bade them goodbye and left relieved of his dilemma.

19

❄

Roman and Sandy lived in the same house though they rarely communicated or were conscious of each other's presence. Their relationship was strained. Roman felt claustrophobic despite the enormous house he lived in. He blamed his father for his failings and wanted to move out as soon as possible. He found a job in a company though the stipend was low because of his low grades, but he was happy that he was employed.

Serendipitously, Shanty was also in the same office, on the same floor, but different designation and at extreme opposite side to that of Roman's cabin. They were at the same place but oblivious to each other.

One afternoon when Shanty was in the canteen having her brunch, she spotted Roman, as he was pulling a chair to take a seat a little away from her table. On seeing him, the flowers of her romance began to bloom again, and the flame of love was rekindled, love tickled her each and every bone, her heart serenaded to the rhythm of unparalleled joy, goose bumps opened up every pore of her body. She felt a thrill of excitement. She quickly veiled her ebullience and walked briskly towards Roman with a nervous smile.

Roman looked up. He had inkling that he had seen her somewhere but had no recollection. Yet he felt an instant cosmic connection.

He was not surrounded by girls anymore and so Shanty gathered the courage to talk to him. She diffidently asked him, "Do you remember me?"

Roman who had just taken a bite of his burger, chewing his mouthful in a gulp wiped the crumbs from his lips and replied, "No Lady. I think we are meeting for the first time."

Shanty reminded him that she used to attend his father's parties regularly. Roman still did not remember but not to make her feel awkward, he politely said, "Yes, yes, of course, come join me at my table."

Shanty knew that Roman really don't have any clue as to who she is, but she wanted to be her friend. This was the ideal moment to get to know each other. While Roman played a guessing game, "If I am right, Are you Sheena"

She said, "No"

He took another guess and blurted out, "Suzy"

She again said, "No"

After two guesses Roman conceded that he has forgotten his name.

Shanty smiled at his goof-ups and said, "Don't embarrass yourself, I know, you don't know my name because we were never introduced."

She extended her hand and said, "My name is Shanty." Roman shook his hand and smiled sheepishly.

They start to talk and continued to meet, sometimes by choice, sometimes by chance.

Past some days Shanty took Roman to her home. Roman asked her, "You said we were neighbors right; then have you shifted residence? Why are you alone? Where are your parents? He wondered.

Shanty waited for Roman to get over the astonishment and then said, "Some years back, both mom and dad were killed in a road mishap."

Roman felt aggrieved for Shanty, he offered his condolences, he remained silent for a moment and then he asked her another question "But you had a big house. We were neighbors then how come you are staying over here?"

Shanty had gone through a tough phase in life; she narrated her family's tragic story, "My father was the first to enter the UK. He slogged day and night; he collected straw by straw and constructed a beautiful mansion. He made arrangements for his brothers to come and settle here to help him manage the prosperous business he had set up."

Roman clasped her hands in his to sympathize with her.

"Dad held tight control over his company's affairs. He would reprimand his brothers on mistakes and malpractices, much to their ire. He did this out of love and so that they could learn and not repeat the mistakes. But they were ungrateful to the love of my father and instead as soon as he died they usurped his business and properties and left me impoverished."

Her voice cracked with a lump in her throat. She dabbed her eyes with a tissue paper and continued, "Suddenly I became orphan, an unwanted orphan, with all the riches gone. It was a tragic end to my fairytale upbringing. I had to start afresh, find a job and rent an apartment."

Roman understood that this was the prime reason for her doing the job. And fate had it that she met her man.

Because of personal tragedies Shanty had lost track of Roman, but had heard about his profligate lifestyle. But the love she felt for him was unflinching and so she forgave him, believing in letting bygones be bygones.

Roman and Shanty became close friends, and sometimes Shanty caught him looking at her with a hint of love in his eyes. She waited for him to propose, but he was hesitant.

After months of courting, he finally popped the question, "Will you….."

And in her excitement she accepted his marriage proposal even before he could complete his sentence; such was her divine love for him. She had no one to seek approval from; she herself took the decision and they got married.

Soon after marriage, Shanty felt that all was not well between father and son. She knew about Roman's past and felt that his father had been a bad influence on him.

The huge house with its empty hollow spaces gave her a feeling of being haunted and she suggested to Roman that they should live separately and meet Sandy occasionally. Thus Shanty; a female, as soon as she came to be the latest resident of the villa, she too shunned the magnanimity in favor of a studio apartment.

Roman had always wanted to move out. At last he had a good reason to leave the house. He left Sandy alone and moved to an apartment that Shanty had rented in the heart of London and away from his father's countryside villa.

The day Roman made his mind to move out; all hell broke loose, as it had done many years ago.

In anger Sandy remarked, "I have heard that in dark times shadow too deserts you. Are you that shadow? What wrong have I done that you have rejected me? I had never stopped you from living the way you wanted to live."

"The only reason I am leaving is because you have never known when to stop. It was your doings that made me stray from path."

"I went back to India to bring you here because of my love for you."

"You are mean and if you had shown some concern for your father, brother or towards my mother, you would not have been alone, I would not be what I am today. Lucky and I would not have left you if you knew how to handle relationships."

All the harm that Sandy had done to his family, the events of his past turned on its head. It happened to him with the same alarming sequences.

He had fought with Swaraj while his father watched helplessly.

Lucky and Roman had fought while he watched helplessly.

When he disappeared, Swaraj was jailed and Siraj was thought to be Swaraj's helper.

Here Lucky ran away, Roman was jailed and he was thought to be co-conspirator.

He had written a letter to Swaraj from a foreign land severing all ties forever.

Lucky had called from a foreign land to sever all ties.

He had gone back to India and so his matter was officially closed.

Lucky came back to testify and Roman was released and the case was closed.

He snubbed Swaraj; dragged Rukmini's hand and left.

Roman was dragging Shanty's hand and was washing his hands of him.

Scenes were repeating themselves with the settings changing.

The images from Sandy's past made a dash and he didn't argue no more.

'Time Changes' 'Time Changes' 'Time changes' 'Time Changes'

The words echoed from all sides in the cavernous and empty hall, their relentless ringing, banging, hammering, reminding and maddening tones brought back the memories and drove him into insanity, abstraction, seclusion, destruction and drowning melancholia.

Roman had completely changed. He had become a responsible husband and gentlemen leaving behind all his happy go lucky days.

The new apartment was tiny compared to the opulence he was used to. And though he was in the hustle-and-bustle of the city away from the serenity of the countryside, Roman whole heartedly adjusted to his new life.

Roman was concerned about his father but averse to bringing him into his life again.

20

❄

Five years later, Roman was having a steady life with nothing major happening. Arun's life was taking strides and galloping like horse. Lucky was now just a passing thought, while Sandy's days of glory had faded away like a winter's sun.

Swaraj consulted Arun about marriage and asked him if he was seeing anyone or was interested in anyone or had any proposal in mind. Arun rather shyly said no.

Swaraj asked for his son's choice before making a choice, the choice he was denied, the choice that he had accepted; the choice he would have accepted anyways and it was a good choice about which he had no qualms.

Now it was his chance to make a choice. Devi and Swaraj had been going through many proposals without Arun's knowledge. They had sifted through many good prospects and had zeroed their choice on a match with a girl from their vicinity called Bhoomi.

Arun met Bhoomi, they formally talked about hobbies and future plans, they glanced at the physical features, they guessed their prospects with their eye movements, they judged by talking skills and overall personality. They performed the routine arrange marriage procedure.

They got engaged for a short period to know their compatibility. Arun liked Bhoomi and she gave him her thumbs-up. And they had an arranged wedding.

Marriage brought good luck and lady luck smiled on him. He was promoted and offered a five years contract to the UK. Arun with Bhoomi left for UK and Swaraj and Devi stayed back.

Arun knew of his father's hidden desire to travel around the world, since the only favor Swaraj had requested from his son was an annual package tour to some foreign country.

Even though he was now comfortably off, Swaraj did not forget Siraj. He helped him set up a small licensed roadside stall selling coconuts outside the gate of jogger's park in his area.

Arun became acclimatized to English weather like duck to the pond; he loved the cool breeze and felt comfortable even to the cold winter and chilly snowfalls. He blended into the work culture and made friends.

He was awed by the infrastructure, the cleanliness, the milieu, the beauty, the splendid Victorian architecture and marvelous modern day structures.

While he was walking along the sidewalk, gazing in amazement at the architectural wonder that had caught his imagination, he accidently bumped into Roman. Roman was holding a cup of coffee that spilled on his shirt with the impact. It was Arun's mistake so even before Roman would react or frown upon him, he profusely apologized. This cooled Roman down and he waved his hands; accepting his apologies. They both moved on. But just after a few steps Arun felt a strange sensation he turned and looked back. Ditto for Roman as he too had the same feeling, he also turned and when their eyes met, they exchanged a smile and walked off in different directions.

Roman mentioned about this to Shanty and Arun discussed the same topic with Bhoomi.

A few months later, it was a fine sunny Sunday afternoon, Arun and Bhoomi had planned a dinner at a café. Shanty pricked Roman to take her on an unplanned dinner to the nearby café. And so coincidently they both were at the same café and at same time.

As always Arun was formally dressed, clean shaven with his hair neatly parted and wearing specs. He looked like a thorough gentleman.

In contrast, Roman came along in long, spunky Bermuda shorts, a flowery beach t-shirt, rugged stubble, unruly hair and put on a black glares. He was cool and casual.

Shanty cursory eyes caught Arun at the distant table and she evaluated the similarity; she was struck by his resemblance to Roman.

Bhoomi excused herself to go to the washroom. Roman was seated at the table near the gate of the washroom, while passing from near his table she too had a look at Roman, she found him to be exactly same to Arun.

They both mentioned to their husbands about the uncanny resemblance. Bhoomi teasingly remarked, "If you come home one day after a fight looking disorderly and disoriented, you will look exactly like the person on that table."

Shanty told Roman the exact opposite that if he dressed soberly he would look exactly like that man.

Both Bhoomi and Shanty observed that the hair whorl, the head structure and even from their back they looked alike.

This aroused their curiosity and they both turned around to have a look.

Roman was seated with his back facing Arun. He tried to lift his neck backwards, but it was too uncomfortable and not worth the effort.

Arun made an attempt but Roman had his back to him and there was a pillar that obstructed his view.

Then the waiter came with the servings and the incident was forgotten.

***

In year 2002, two years after Arun had been in the UK, he became a proud father to a son, Bhoomi delivered a boy.

Roman would occasionally visit Sandy.

Sandy's debts had piled up and could never be repaid. His treasure had emptied, the first to go were the artifacts, then the paintings, the centre table and the mahogany sofa set, the intricate pieces of furniture, the silken rugs, the chandeliers, the cars and then the remaining shares and bonds.

The aquarium was gone with the fish dead due to neglect and decay; if the master was decaying who would bother for the poor fish. The last to go was butler. Sandy had taken care of him and had never ill treated or abused him and he had responded after his master. But his services were becoming a burden on Sandy's expenses so he released him.

His condition was deteriorating day by day. He had lost all his will to live. His health had taken a beating.

Sandy's only fading hope was to see the face of Roman's child. He would always ask Roman when he would give him the good news, but Roman was unable to reply whenever he raised the issue. They had been trying to start the family but with little luck. Roman was trying but not able to conceive. Finally they decided to visit a doctor. The tests on the couple were conducted at a best fertility clinic in the country, and to their dismay and horror, the result that they received was shocking and unbelievable.

The doctor gave the all's well result to Shanty's fertility chances but pointed the finger towards Roman's ability. Roman was not satisfied with the result, so with hope he went for a recheck.

The doctor asked Roman "What kind of a past lifestyle did you live?"

Roman answered honestly "I had slept with many girls, I had taken all kinds of drugs, had pot and grass and had a carefree sex life. I used contraceptives and was confident of my ability to become father whenever I pleased, I was guilt free."

The specialist doctor summarized his problem "I have gone through your reports and medical history. I have just this to say that 'use is a need but when you abuse, it becomes crime.' You abused your body, the drug overdose destroyed you internally, and it has reduced the sperm count that has rendered you sterile."

Roman when he had been encountered with the truth had tears in his eyes. He covered his face in despair and shame.

He told Shanty, "It is for my fault that you are suffering."

Shanty told him, "At the time when you were a spoilt brat; even at that time too you were my hero. The next time when we met after a long hiatus and when I found you a changed man, you rose in my eyes from a Hero to Superhero."

"I am not worth of your affection. I am a bad person, I am a bad husband. If you want you can leave for a family life with children that I would not be able to guarantee. I had thought that producing a child was in my hands. But I have been paid for my sins." cried Roman.

"A person is a bad person if he keeps on making mistakes and does not repent. A person is a bad person if he does mistakes and keeps on repeating it. A bad person is the one who stands by his mistakes and a bad person is the one who is not ashamed of his mistakes. But you have redeemed yourself, you have changed for the better, you have accepted your mistakes. So you are my hero and I am proud of you."

"Don't worry; nowadays we have many options such as in-vitro fertilization, surrogate motherhood or an easy option of adoption. So don't lose heart and I am not going to lose you after winning you." She held Roman in her arms, gave a tight embrace, laid her head on his shoulders, smiled and comforted him.

The honest analyze was like a thorn that had pierced Roman's heart. He realized that his past waywardness had cost him dearly. He accepted the verdict of his destiny. But Shanty didn't break down with the news; she stood like a pillar of strength during this heart wrenching period of Roman's life.

21

⁂

Swaraj was at ease with life. The last few years had changed his fortunes and destiny. The riches had brought him status and the package tour every year was like an icing on a cake. His wish of exploring the world, visiting new places, meeting people, observing their way of life, appreciating the beauty of nature, learning about language and culture had been fulfilled. In a short time he had made up for the lost years when he was a porter.

Arun had been in the UK for four years and now had two children, a daughter and a son. He didn't want any more children and so he had a vasectomy operation.

During those four years Swaraj and Devi had gone globe-trotting, covering almost half of the world. They had visited Australia and New Zealand. Indonesia, Malaysia Singapore, Thailand, Hong-kong in South East Asia, Oman, Qatar, Bahrain, Kuwait, Israel, United Arab Emirates in the Middle-east, South Africa, Seychelles, Madagascar and Maldives exploring the African cape and islands. In-between the year they would make several pilgrimage tours within India.

It was Arun's last year in the United Kingdom and he arranged for a Schengen visa so that his parents could visit Europe with the UK as their final destination. They would stay with his family for some time before they embarked on their return journey to India together.

Towards the end of his stay, Arun had an interesting encounter with destiny. In the last five years he had been regularly promoted and was now overseeing the auctions of confiscated and mortgaged properties of banks, which have run into default on collateral arrangement or had been declared insolvent.

One day at office, a letter was lying on his table that made him revisit his past in a flash. He was given charge of the foreclosure of a property that listed the address as '52, William Villa, Harrow, HA-2, 1BA, London, United Kingdom and defaulter's name was Sandy Keeshun Goswamy.

It sent alarm bells ringing through his mind. His mind began to swirl as he made attempts to find the connection to the address.

Devi had given Arun a copy of the Gita and had instructed him to make sure that it always remained with him.

He rushed home and opened the Gita and found the envelope he had tucked away many years ago. The envelope was in its place intact, crisp and pressed. And bingo, the address was the same.

The company for which Roman worked was engaged in purchasing auctioned properties on behalf of clients. The company would form a team of four to five employees, who would record each and every detail of the property to be purchased and reserve a buyable price. Roman was the leader of the group and as it happened, the property to be purchased turned out to be his villa.

Thus, it was for the first time that Arun as an indirect seller on behalf of the auction house, Roman as a purchaser on behalf of his client and Sandy whose property was at stake, came face to face.

Auction day arrived.

A large shamiana had been set up in the spacious garden of the villa as protection from the sun and to provide shade. A platform had been erected, there was a long table and a chair and on the side a dais had been placed with a hammer and gong on it, the instruments displaying their importance to the affairs of the day.

Opposite to it, chairs cloaked with satin covers, were placed in rows. It was an elaborate and perfectly arranged afternoon auction under Arun's observation.

On the morning of the auction Arun was given the additional charge of carrying out the auction. Previously he had just been an observer. Inadvertently it was Arun hammering the last nail in Sandy's empty coffers.

Arun faced the audience. Roman was seated in the middle row with his client and colleagues, planning strategies, sharing tips and engrossed in discussions about the possible limit to be quoted.

Sandy sat on the last seat of the last row, dispirited, awaiting his downfall, watching the action of auction taking place in the garden of his villa.

Arun had known that this property was of his uncle's. He knew what the job was all about and what he was supposed to do. He was vacillating a bit, remorseful about what he had to do but at the same time he was delighted when he thought of what his uncle had done to his father.

Roman knew his house. He was quoting the price, raising the stakes, but the competition was heating up and Roman felt he was losing his hold on the deal. He had kept a trump card under his sleeve, and now was the time to play his trump card. He employed his ploy; he threw an ace in the ring.

A person stood up and argued with Arun that the auction house had veiled crucial information about the house; that it had a long history of repulsion to women presence, the villa was indeed haunted.

This little revelation played its part. The fellow bidders; the gathering and even the auction house were stunned as they all were unaware of this hidden information, but this ploy worked and there and then the competitors submitted their bids.

As Roman was representing a gay couple and the fact of the house being haunted was known only to Sandy and Roman, the revelation worked in Roman's favour.

The auction house was ready to make a deal at the last quoted price to whoever was interested; Roman clinched the deal for his client by paying the exact price that he had reserved as the best buying price. Roman did not let anybody know that it was his own house. He acted professionally.

Sandy watching everything from behind was proud of Roman's strategy of closing the deal with the help of his bait. A sign of his becoming expert in his field and dedicated to his job; at the same time he was shattered at his personal loss.

After the auction, the three of them met for the first time. Roman and Arun remembered their chance meeting, on the roadside, where they had accidently bumped and so they greeted each other warmly, but they were still unnerved by their resemblance to each other. However, they would soon be aware of their relationship.

Arun Swaraj Goswami, his full name had already made Sandy suspicious about his identity, so when the auction was in its full flow, he fastidiously found out a bit more about Arun. He had discovered that he was his brother's son.

Arun already knew who Sandy was and greeted him with sympathy for the loss of his villa, though due to business protocol; he had to conceal his identity.

Roman didn't want to meet Sandy. He had covered up his identity from his client and colleagues; moreover even though he was concerned about Sandy, his commitment lay with his wife and new life. He did not want his father to re-enter his settled life and so he left quickly after the auction.

But by then they knew that they were cousins.

Arun saw Roman leaving hurriedly and his mind started to swim in the pool of questions, 'Why did Roman get involved with clients to sell his own home?'

'Why didn't Roman and Sandy talk?'

'Why is their relationship strained?'

'How did his uncle got so rich?'

'And now, what was the reason for his uncle's downfall?' etc.....

When everyone had left Arun returned to Sandy to get his unsolved mysteries answered. Sandy was still over there sitting conscience-stricken. Arun was startled when Sandy immediately hugged him tightly.

Sandy remarked, "Even though you didn't reveal your identity, your name interested me. You have come back to me with questions in your eyes and this makes me realize that you know about my identity as well."

Arun nodded

"Do you want to know the story behind my present circumstances?"

He again nodded without uttering a word.

Sandy started to tell Arun the story from the days he came to Britain to his present situation. Hours past by and the bright afternoon turned into dull evening. Arun felt no emotions, but seeing his uncle in need, he assured him of his help.

When Arun got up to leave Sandy added, "The difference between your father and me is that your father lived for his family and lost everything for his family. On the other hand, I lived for myself and lost everything because of my deeds and my family."

On hearing this Arun chest swelled with the pride of being Swaraj's son. He left with a smile.

Sandy had no money, no family and no place to go. The auction house made arrangements with the social security services to take care of him, providing him with monthly reimbursement to deal with his daily and medical needs.

Sandy was a loser and his life was worthless. His only companion was a bottle in hand and deep thoughts in his mind. His drunkenness took its toll on his health. The security service staff tried their best to reform him but to no avail.

Sandy longed for Mini's companionship. He had discarded her from his life and in all these years, he had never bothered to contact her. But desperate time calls for desperate measures, he had the copies of the agreement for the house he had purchased for her in Bombay, and so he got in touch with her.

Mini had always been a carrying wife with traditional Indian values where the husband is regarded as god. When she heard about his plight she was more than willing to take care of him and let him into her life again.

Sandy made up his mind to leave Britain and move in with Mini. Sandy gathered all his documents and prepared to bid UK goodbye once and forever. Mini also filed her papers to go to Sandy and bring him along.

But before he could take another step, destiny decided his future for him. He collapsed one day and was hospitalized. The search for his family led the staff to Mini. They contacted her immediately and she left India at once.

Sandy's liver had ruptured beyond repair and his kidneys had failed. His condition had become too critical for him to survive.

Sandy now knew about Swaraj and his good times. Ironically, he was in the midst of his bad times, fighting his battle with life, alone.

The words again started to ring in his ears: 'TIME-CHANGES'.

Roman came to know about Sandy's condition and reached the hospital. Mini too had arrived but by that time Sandy had passed away.

Mother and son met in the hospital's lobby.

Roman performed the last rites for Sandy. After the cremation, Roman took Mini home. They talked about their past years and got to know more about each other. Mini being a mother was concerned about Lucky's well being to which Roman said "It's our bad luck that he is no more in contact with us and is ignorant about his father's death, but I have a gut feeling that he is safe and happy, wherever he is.

Mini tried to convince Roman to move his base to India, as it was the place to be at present. Roman weighed the pros and cons of relocating. He was earning well but had no savings. He did not own a house and was living in a rented apartment in obnoxiously expensive London.

Shanty having spent her formative years in India liked and missed its culture and social fabric and she was more than willing to relocate.

He applied for a job and got a plum offer in a MNC, less on his grades but more on the basis of having a foreign degree and experience of working in a foreign country. His earnings would be at par with what he currently earned but with substantial savings and with the standard of living being very nominal compared to London, he would be able to enjoy a luxurious life. He preferred to shift.

Arun by that time had arranged for Swaraj and Devi's visit to UK on vacation a part of his commitment to a yearly package tour.

Swaraj before setting out wanted to take Bhoomi a gift as it is customary for guests to carry something with them when they visit somebody's home. And after all he was going to his own house and to his own daughter-in-law. He bought two designer bangles and a gold coin.

He arrived at Arun's home laden with toys, clothes, homemade food stuffs for his grandchildren and presented Bhoomi with two bangles.

Arun was eager to share the developments of last few days. He told his father about his meeting with Sandy and Roman. He wanted the two brothers to meet. Besides, he had assured Sandy that he would help him. But when they went to Roman's office they were confronted to the reality that he had left the company and had probably relocated to India. They also learned that his father has died.

Sandy and Swaraj were never able to meet in this life.

Swaraj was disappointed when he heard the news, years of no connect had made Swaraj somewhat practical so he missed his brother but it did not stir his emotions, he took the news of Sandy's death in his stride and commenced on another mission. To find the lady who had once presented him with a gold coin. The only clue he had was the jewelry box with her firm's name and address engraved on it.

But then with such a vital clue it was not difficult to locate her. The lady's business had grown in stature but her appearance hadn't changed much, only the age was catching up on her.

He went to his store and fixed a meeting with her. He reminded her of her good deed which she had long forgotten. He told her his full story. She was wonderstruck by Swaraj's upsurge.

Swaraj and Devi stayed for three months in London and then returned to India with Arun's family.

22

❋

Swaraj returned to his normal schedule and work as the housing society's secretary.

It was mid-May. The summer was at its height. Arun was uncomfortable with this sudden change in climate and especially so for Roman who had also shifted to India, he felt like he had been thrown into a boiling pot from the cool climbs of London, the heat of summer was too much for his liking; he found it difficult initially. But as Arun re-adjusted so did Roman adjusted.

May heat wave had slowed down the movements of people on the road; Siraj at his coconut stall was waiting for customers, when he came across an unusual customer who had stopped by to drink coconut water. She was a middle-aged lady dressed in tight jeans and sweat shirt, branded sport shoes, with headphones and walkman in her hand. She was a typical urban lady.

When Siraj was a young man and when he would go to his village from Bombay, Siraj being a fashionista, he would don a look of a 1980's hero and had his own style statement with well parted and oiled hair, a clean-shaven face and big side locks. He would be smartly dressed with colorful shirts and bell bottomed pants.

But as of today he was a changed man, he had a skull cap on his tonsured head, now the hairs had exchanged their setting. From clean-shaved face now it was a clean-shaved head and in place of long black hair on his head it was a long flowing salt and pepper beard. Pant and shirt had been replaced by kurta-pyjama. In his new avatar he could be easily mistaken for a nearby mosque's Imam.

Siraj remembered those old days when he would visit Swaraj's home there he would see Rukmini always been clad in a sari, with her head covered and with the shyness of a newly-wed bride. She would never raise her eyes not even her voice.

The women in front of her had the same distinctive affinity. But the sari had been replaced by western wear, veiled head by unbound hair.

Not confident yet he tentatively asked, 'Rukmini your coconut'

Mini was taken aback; she looked stunningly at Siraj as she herself had forgotten her real name after years of being known as Mini. Mini's exposure to the outside world, knowledge of English, self confidence and resolve to do something fruitful inspired her to be innovative.

With passage of time she had earned a name, respect, prestige, status in society and was now a successful businesswoman. Thus she had a changed appearance. She was now Madam Mini.

She had correctly guessed the person in front of her. He was Mr. Siraj, a known person from her old days. She had left her past behind and moved ahead. She had never expected to bump into her past again but this chance meeting changed her perception – it was indeed a small world.

Rukmini said, "Yes Siraj bhai it's me Rukmini. But you can call me Mini."

Rukmini received a call on her mobile and she excused herself to talk on the phone, Siraj observed that the tongue-tied Rukmini had become a chirping bird. And whisper in her voice had changed into one of authority.

Rukmini came back to the stall, picked up the coconut, had a sip while Siraj said; "I know that Sandeep is dead, Rohan your elder son is settled in India and you have another son Lucky somewhere in USA. But where on earth you were was a mystery."

Rukmini said, "I also know about Swaraj bhai and about his family through Rohan but we are still to meet. Now that we have met, I want our meeting to remain a secret till it's an appropriate time to meet them."

Mini uncovered the story of her transformation; she began, "After my break up with Sandy, I returned to India, I severed all ties with my old world, I decided to begin afresh. Bombay was where I preferred to live. I had some savings of pound sterling, a pocketful of gold, an apartment, loneliness and the only skill of culinary in my kitty.

To kill my time, I got involved in trying out new recipes, to keep myself busy I started with a Tiffin service. The food was delicious and the word spread. I started receiving orders in bulk. I hired a helper and started making pickles and poppadums, I left the work of preparing to the helper and ventured into the market to sell it."

"I was a simple salesgirl like all others, but I had an advantage. That advantage was, I was able to talk English fluently. This proved to be a special key that opened many doors for me. When I conversed in English my persona made an impression. The respect given to me increased many-folds. My aggressive marketing, quality product and the mere knowledge of a foreign language earned me orders."

"You put your skills to good use" said Siraj and Mini smiled and continued.

"With the skill the luck too smiled on me. The orders kept on getting bigger and bigger by the day and the apartment from where I began; began to look congested and constrained. I sold all my gold, mortgaged the apartment and converted all the pounds into handsome amount of rupees. And with the money I started a cottage industry, and diversified the product range by introducing sweets, ready to eat recipes, jams, ketchup, sherbets. The business started to flourish. I catered to the Indian diaspora and became a manufacturer-cum-exporter.

"I was alone and I didn't need a big space to live. So I divided my workplace into two; one half as a factory and another as my cozy little room. I employed only women as per my work requirements.

Working with them I became aware of their daily problems and the women related issues: women fighting their in-laws against dowry harassments or harassment after giving birth to a female child, women dealing with abusive husbands, irresponsible husband, alcoholic husbands and all sorts of domestic violence. I began to counsel them and then more and more cases began to come to me. Acid-attacks, threat of honor killings for inter-caste and inter-religion marriages. I fought for their cases pro bono because I believe in women's rights."

"Years passed by, the business grew by leaps and bounds. I now have a sea-facing apartment and a family too." She added, "Yes Roman and Shanty are in-fact living with me."

Siraj was impressed. He saluted her purpose, her achievement and her spirit.

Mini and Siraj talked for long time making up for lost years. Their meeting opened up a Pandora's Box.

Siraj came to know that Rukmini lived in the same locality and she came to the park once a day, either in the morning or evening, to exercise and jog. Now she would stop at his stall and exchange greetings.

***

It was July the 25th of year 2005.

The torrential downpour by nature had created havoc in the city of Mumbai, flooding it and exposing the loopholes in the management of the richest municipality of India.

Siraj's shop was submerged and his small scale investment was washed off. Swaraj was by his side to offer him his help in his hour of need.

After the water level subsided they both had tea at nearby tea stall and their discussions began over the deplorable infrastructure of one of the most advanced and populated metro.

Swaraj "If I would have wanted I would have helped you erect an unauthorized stall anywhere on a busy public encroached property. But we went through a legal tender procedure and put a stall outside the garden at an authorized place."

Siraj cut him short, "How an encroached unauthorized stall would have helped?"

"Have you heard about Mithi River in Mumbai, it acts as a storm drain River; it carries the excess rainwater into Arabian Sea. But go and have a look at it. Nowadays it drains sewage, industrial waste, animal waste and organic waste. The river has shrunken in width with mangroves being cut and encroachments being built. And then when such phenomenal rain batters the city the city is gifted with polluted water. This all is the result of corruption. The authorities are turning a blind eye to illegal constructions and are making merry with the connivance of officers and land grabbers.

This is blocking the natural path of the water and clogging the drainage and this is the reason the city gets flooded."

"So you mean that we too should have erected an illegal stall."

"Don't take it literally. I mean to say is can you see even the sign of foot-paths. They are claimed by all and sundry. We go the straight-way and we are fixed for good. They walk the crooked path and do not suffer a bit.

Therefore I feel there is no use walking a straight path." Swaraj lamented.

As Swaraj has toured many cities around the world, he continued, "British Raj was not that bad; after all the drainage system in Mumbai was set up by them and no major changes had been done to it since Independence.

I recently visited Hong-kong and I can say from my personal experience. It remained UK's colony for far too long and see the infrastructure of that city to believe it. I feel British Raj would have been beneficial to us, they would have developed our cities like Hong-kong, checked corruption and controlled our population explosion, because when they left, India's population stood at 40 crores and since then we have added God knows how many crores. We feel proud to be the second most populated country in the world. Perhaps that has been our distinctive achievement." He said sarcastically.

They sat for a long time, with Swaraj in his full flow indulged in tirade and banter, sipping a cup after cup of tea, while the windy rains battered the sea side Mumbai. And when it was late in the evening, Swaraj waved a goodbye and departed towards his home.

23

❋

It was celebration time, 15th August the day of India's Independence was nearing.

Arun asked Siraj to come to the house to help plan Swaraj's birthday along with Independence-day by arranging a party at the home keeping it a private family affair.

Siraj came to Swaraj's place one day prior on 14th August to decorate the house for the function, the next day.

The day indeed turned out to be a day of breaking news.

Early in the morning before Siraj came, Arun broke the first news, Arun had undergone vasectomy the operation which is considered nearly foolproof but he fell into accidental category and Bhoomi was impregnated with their third child. Arun waveringly, broke the news to his family.

When Siraj arrived he brought them a bigger surprise. He adjudicated this to be an appropriate time to talk about Sandy's family whom he was in contact with for the last few months. He narrated the full episode of his meetings with Rukmini and her family.

Swaraj, Devi, Bhoomi, Arun all stalled their work and in apt attention listened to Siraj.

Arun spoke "So that was the reason we had lost touch with Roman whom we were searching in an alien country, when he was so near to us, almost in our backyard"

After a long pause the ladies of the house again got busy with kitchen duties while the men with a male servant proceeded with their work of embellishing the hall area with festoons, silver-golden shining stripes, balloons, paper Indian flags, ribbon wands by tying, nailing, gluing and shuttling up and down the long stool, engaged in the work and enjoying hot and spicy samosas, sandwiches and chutney; all the while they watched television, when suddenly all of them were glued to the television, this time the media came up with a Breaking news.

The news channel flashed an impromptu 'Breaking News' of death of popular Indian politician named 'Babulal'.

Swaraj and Siraj exchanged glances with their minds revisiting their past immediately.

Babulal had influenced Swaraj's life he was the purchaser of his land, his only ray of hope in need, his money bank. His whole land now belonged to Babulal. Swaraj's farmland had now become his farmhouse. His dilapidated house refurbished, refurnished and renovated into a palatial farmhouse cottage. As the city was only at the distance of 20 kilometers, the outskirts of village where Swaraj had his land had now become the suburbs of modern developing city. The land rates of the area had skyrocketed to phenomenal levels.

Babulal all his life did his own good, his own upliftment using his caste tag and his caste people as vote bank to succeed. The irony of his death was; his death day was declared as 'Uthan diwas' or 'Upliftment Day'. The news was carried by every news channel.

Dispersing, they again got back working towards what they had gathered for. Siraj bid them goodbye hoping to meet tomorrow.

Arun had taken a day off to see after the preparation, catering, decoration and had been busy all the while gathering information about Lucky as he was the only missing leaf of Kisna's family tree. After hours of search on social networking sites, he chanced upon his current status, which stated that he was presently in India with his so called partner in search of his roots, appealing anybody to share any information.

Arun contacted him, he just told him that he had an important information and for that to be shared they would need to meet, he fixed the meeting point the next day at his house, with the intention of ending Lucky's search and arranging him to meet all his relatives under one roof. Lucky was invited to the party, detached of what's in store.

Swaraj knew that the computer has the brain power of humans, memory storage of human, competence level of humans, but by giving it a human touch, by finding the lost at the click of a mouse was truly a marvelous achievement of the device of the century, century of Computer Age. He was astounded at the advancement of technology. He saluted the invention of Computers.

At dining table Bhoomi, Devi, Swaraj and Arun had a long conversation regarding tomorrow's preparation, the same time they discussed about Roman and Lucky.

Swaraj advocated an idea that "As Rohan is termed medically unfit to reproduce, I want to unburden him of his tragedy and give him the joy of fatherhood and family, if Arun and Bhoomi have any objection, they discuss among themselves tonight and if they agree, we will propose Rohan to adopt Arun's to be born third child".

***

The D-day arrived, the party began. The guest started to pour in. The first person to enter was Siraj with his family and that of Sandeep's with Rukmini, Rohan and Shanti. Swaraj and Sandeep's family greeted warmly with tears of joy flowing, no explanation was needed of their changed looks, changed circumstances, changed fortunes and changed times, Siraj as an intermediary had cleared the air from both sides.

The bigger surprise entry next was of Nirmala and Shrishti. Nirmala had shifted to Mumbai and was living with Shrishti, she was now a reputed gynecologist in best city hospital, Nirmala was head mistress of a government school.

The hard work of Nirmala had paid off and her confrontation with in-laws and determination to prove that both sexes are equal had paid dividends.

Shrishti was flooded with marriage proposals with groom families granting dowry instead of demanding, the female feticide had being one of the prime reasons for the reverse trend.

Shrishti being a gynecologist was involved in the noble cause of saving a girl child. She was still a spinster though she was of Arun's age, breaking yet another taboo that the girls should be married of or say discarded off at the earliest.

Everyone entered the party everyone exchanged pleasantries; some were meeting after eons. Everyone was eager to listen as well as share their life stories. They got busy in conversation; the party was in full flow, the room was buzzing with clamor.

There was knocking at the door and to everybody's surprise the latest entrant was Lucky with a stranger. Rohan was shell shocked at seeing Lucky. Lucky was joyous and dumb, to see him.

Arun dispersed the air of confusion and explained everything. Rohan and Lucky were profound as they both hugged and embraced tightly.

Lucky, forget the roots found the complete family tree. He was introduced to all family members.

They cut the cake and celebrated Swaraj's birthday and Independence Day by fluttering the flag on the window sill.

Arun knew that there were many stories to be heard, many stories to be told. He had requested the guests to say something about Swaraj and his (its) impact on their lives. First to come was Siraj

He is a bore, when he talks he owns no sense of humor, he behaves like a grand dad, he likes to put sense into everyone, he thinks of himself as a guru, like to talk in platitudes, his verses have the waft of verbosity, his circumlocutory speeches about everything is too much to bear for my helpless soul. But jokes apart, he has this distinct ability to hold tight relations and friendship, ability to guide, ability to give, ability to rise from ruins and his ability to make me too believe in his concept that 'Time-changes.'

I was born the same year as Swaraj, but have a go at my passport, my ration card, my birth certificate, my all other government documents all claim to have me born on any given date depending on the whim of the officer, this is the case with half of the population born during that period and it would have been the case with Swaraj too but he was born to be remembered, destined to witness his growth with that of the nation. As he came out of the darkness of his life into the sunshine, so has the nation.

I am proud to be part of Swaraj's life and Independent India.

Next, Nirmala took the centre stage

Right from cradle under the care of Swaraj, I know his importance in my life, the importance of Independence; importance of being independent, confident of taking decisions aware of the backing of Swaraj. For me independence barring few bumps had been a smooth ride. My divorce opened my way towards self-dependence. India's divorce from British Raj helped it to be self-reliant.

Next to make the way to the centre was Shrishti

Uncle Swaraj had been what

Uncle Sam is to Americans.

They are prospering under its shelter. I prospered under him.

India has come out of its infancy into adulthood this has been the best phase of its growth. Youthfulness is the backbone of the thriving nation. Youth with it bring energy, vitality, dare-devilry, intensity, ideas, innovation, implementation, awe, admire, inspiration and growth. We are in our prime so is our nation.

Thanks to Swaraj, Thanks to Independence. Three cheers to Swaraj. Three cheers to the feeling of being Independent.

She handed the baton to his uncle Swaraj for a final say.

Swaraj had put in a great effort and penned down the summary of his life intertwining with the events of India, with letter of thanksgiving. When Swaraj speaks, he is very witty for anybody to ignore him, so each and every soul took their place and sat down intriguingly, there was pin drop silence. Swaraj started his sermon (oops, speech).

The day I was born, the same day India was born. It was 58 years ago. Both Swaraj have seen many ups and downs, the best thing is both have survived, fought their downs and are settling in their new roles, enjoying their ups, trying to improve and looking forward towards better tomorrow.

Today I am watching the rising and thriving middle class, the rise in soft power of service sector, the growth of urban areas and I am happy to be part of this growth. Today the likes of Arun, Shrishti and young generation are creating wealth, elevating their families to rise from poverty to self sufficiency.

The inflation in land rates have bulged past the year 2000; thereby increasing the middle class, making millionaires the farmers with land near the ever expanding urban centers, decreasing the gap between urban and rural areas.

My land that I sold for a pittance have now turned into gold mine, it is my personal loss.

Urbanization has increased migration to cities; it is a sign of progress and paradigm shift of Indian economic dependence from agriculture to service sector. I, Siraj, Nirmala and many others are examples of this shift.

Nirmala's resolute to get herself educated and independent by overcoming many odds and obstacles, progress of Shrishti in education, the sign of women power of new emerging India. Rukmini's surprise rise is again an eye opener of success through determination.

Sandeep's family's return to India, Mini, Roman again becoming Rukmini and Rohan likewise of our Bombay again becoming Mumbai back to the original. Rohan migrating to India is the signal of Brain gain, gone are the days of Brain drain. A welcome sign of India's effort to become economic power house. And we have accepted Lucky and his partner into our family. Surely we as a family have progressed to accept the relation that even now some view as taboo.

He pointed towards his servant and said "The person standing in the corner is not to be mistaken as our servant. He is no less than my son. His name is Aftab, he is one who saved and took care of Arun during riots. This is the minimum that I can do to show my gratitude. Aftab is to Arun what Siraj is to me. One and one makes eleven, to take India on the path of progress Siraj and Swaraj both 'Raj' have to work in tandem.

If it was British Raj before 1947 it has to be Si'Raj' and Swa'Raj' now and forever. Our friendship should be slap on the face of politicians for whom we are not Indians but meager vote banks.

Swaraj looked towards Arun, Arun nodded, and Swaraj announced, "Here again I would like to put forward an offer to Roman, if he is willing to adopt Arun's child," saying so he broke the news of Bhoomi's pregnancy to one and all.

Rohan without a blink or second thoughts instantly agreed. Swaraj once again showed his big heartedness by completing Rohan's family, by bringing together and closer two cousins, by displaying the traces of his altruist nature, that even after so many years of separation and Sandeep's indifferent attitude towards him, he still cared for his family.

The irony was Sandeep wanted the best for his family by ignoring Swaraj, but the destiny made his son Rohan to adopt Swaraj's grandchild, thus bringing the life to full circle.

Everyone present were stunned and marveled at the depth of Swaraj speech, they were moved and inspired, proud to be part of the family and above all being an Indian.

The deft silence was broken by Siraj's applauding and everybody joining in.

They all stood up, applauded, cheered, hooted and then stood in attention reciting the National Anthem.

'Jana Gana Mana ....